MW01252528

Olympic National Park, the Wild Side

Daniel Hance Page

PTP
PTP Book Division
Imprint of Saguaro Books, LLC
Arizona

PTP Book Division
An Imprint of Saguaro Books, LLC
16845 E. Avenue of the Fountains, Ste.325
Fountain Hills, AZ 85268
www.ptpbookdivision.com

ISBN: 9798363634482
Library of Congress Cataloging Number
LCCN: 2022950790
Printed in the United States of America
First Edition

Dedication

Marg, Hank, Jim, Ivadelle, Sheldon, Colleen, Shane, and Shannon Page, John, Dan, and the Robinson family, Lester and Rose Anderson, Doug, Don, Bob Sephton and families, Garry and the Pratt family, the Massey family, Murray, Sue, and the Shearer family, Joe and Linda Hill, Macari Bishara, Joan LeBoeuf, Kevin, Alison, and Michaela Griffin, Jerry and Gaye McFarland, Dr. David and June Chambers, "Mac" McCormick, Grant Sanders, Frank Lewis and other friends with whom we have enjoyed the wilderness

Left to right: Jim Page (Writer's brother), John Robinson (Friend), Dan Robinson (John's son), Dan Page (Writer)

Other Books by Daniel Hance Page

Killbear Park, the Wild Side
Smoky Mountains, the Wild Side
Yellowstone, the Wild Side
Banff, the Wild Side
Return of the Wild
Florida Journeys
Pelican Sea, a Legend of Florida
Walk Upon the Clouds, a Legend of the Rocky Mountains
The Pirate and the Gunfighter
The First Americans and Their Achievements
Life is a Fishing Trip
Riley, the Dog Visitor
Bear Trap Mountain
Where Wilderness Lives
Many Winters Past
The Journey of Jeremiah Hawken
Told by the Ravens
The Maui Traveler
Wilderness Trace
Arrowmaker
Trail of the River
Pelican Moon
Legend of the Uintas

When we try to pick out anything by itself, we find it hitched to everything else in the universe.

John Muir 1911

Chapter 1

The Three Lives of Gray Raven

1860

Gray Raven's early life was a time of happiness and he shone this light into the lives of other people. His qualities included appearance women liked and strength men respected. He had high status in the Quinault village not only because of his family but, also, through the prospect of what his abilities would contribute. He was intelligent and tried to see life as an opportunity rather than just a burden. He wore the same clothing as other men and kept his hair long, though tied in place with a strand of cedar bark.

The Quinault village, where Gray Raven lived was located in an area that, in the future, would become part of Olympic National Park. As motionless as rocks beside him, he greeted a new day. Resting on a ridge of dry sand, he looked westward while the rising sun in the east shot rays of golden light through misty vastness where power flowed in the form of long swells. One after another out of darkness, now receiving light, swells moved toward the land, curled upward, caught golden rays from the sun then fell with a thundering boom, sending water rushing in a bubbling mass to and along shore. Their power spent, the flows swirled back to rejoin the sea.

Water has power, beauty and mystery that I greet at the start of each day, thought Gray Raven. *Behind me are forests equally great as are the mountains, which complete the power of the world where we live. Surrounded by such vastness, people can connect with it, see they are part of it and each unique individual can contribute to life. Separate from the Spirit connecting all life, some people without success seek to be important. My strength lies in seeing the light of life at an early age.*

Having greeted the new day, Gray Raven walked to his place in the long house, gathered equipment including bow and arrows then started his usual journey to the mountains. Following paths and ridges he knew well, he climbed upward, always moving higher. He looked down at the river, now appearing to be only a shining line glimmering along a base of rock walls. Looking into such a deep canyon, he noticed the air, usually unseen, now took on a presence, being a shimmering, bluish colored substance. *Air is thick,* he observed. *It can help to hold birds, even eagles, and is particularly strong when whirling.*

When a rock he stepped on moved, he dislodged it with his foot, sending a large slab over the edge, starting a clattering sound that dropped into silence disturbed only by a slight breeze brushing against rock walls. *That could be my life if I'm not careful,* he warned himself. *I must not become careless or overly confident about my abilities. Only*

11

mountain goats and a dwindling number of sheep live here, along with those held aloft by movement of air, such as eagles and ravens. I should greet them only in my spirit.

Gray Raven climbed to another ridge where it opened to a wider area. He waited. Clouds moved below him. Near his side, an eagle soared. Yellow eyes watched him.

The mountain goats arrived. In single file the white-coated animals walked into the open area just before Gray Raven shot one arrow then another. One ram fell as the others moved out of sight.

Gray Raven started working. He saved the hide then used it as a carrying container for the meat. Remnant parts were left on the ridge. The rest of the day went past while he carried the precious supplies to a camp he had made beside the river.

Water splashing over a pebbly riverbed provided a background sound as company for Gray Raven while he sat within warmth of a fire. Ram meat roasted on slender poles above the flames.

Mountain goats are a majestic part of life in the mountains, mused Gray Raven after he tasted a first chunk of roasted meat and found it to be as tender as it was flavorful. *Some goats can be used for food and blankets while the others continue to live and add their place where all parts are joined together as one, spiritually. Only together are we powerful. I can remove goats for necessities as long as I don't take too many.*

Following the meal, he extended the top of his shelter to protect half of the fire because thunder was rumbling, indicating approaching rain. Strikes of thunder became louder while the sky clouded, darkening the landscape. At first a few drops of rain fell then it poured in a white sheet of hissing spray splashing around the shelter with its protected fire.

"That's an unusual sight," exclaimed Gray Raven, when he saw a brown bear wade into the river. Following the mother, two cubs came. All three chased salmon. The mother caught a fish in her jaws. The salmon struggled, moving both head and tail but the jaws held and carried the catch to a gravel bank where the cubs started eating. The mother returned to the stream and brought out two more fish, supplying a feast. When the bears finished eating they walked farther downstream.

I feel everywhere at home except in my village, mused Gray Raven. *I'm home now in company of the spiritual presence of the Creator providing power of the ocean, forest and mountains. I greet these special places every day and recognize their strength. I seek visions with their messages of understanding into and from life beyond what we see. There is only one Creator providing a common link to all other individual spirits. I'm never alone. In spirit, I'm tied to all parts of life and each person is offered the same comfort, although some people don't accept it and turn their backs to the spiritual side of life*

Following the meal, Gray Raven added the cooking sticks to the fire. He walked to the stream, drank some of the cold, clear water then returned to sit and enjoy the warmth and light of the fire. It seemed to become brighter as the surrounding landscape darkened amid gathering shadows of evening. Soon there was only the fire and its dancing light to brighten the night.

In my young life, I've been lucky, thought Gray Raven. *I have sufficient talents to make me useful and a leader among people. I don't have to seek people for companions because they come to me and look for my company or help. I get status from what I can actually contribute and through potential gifts I will give in the future. I like to not just live but try to understand life. Maybe I think too much but being part of what is happening is not where the true excitement lies buried. Life becomes more incredible in not just seeing the way things are but in looking beyond into the spiritual world where there is to be discovered why things are, and why it's all worth our efforts. I know nobody lives in vain, except those who travel only for themselves. Each one is to struggle to be the best they can be, seeing each obstacle not as a burden but an opportunity to hone the spirit against the test of troubles that exists only here and not in the realm of real life of the spiritual world.*

The next morning, Gray Raven carried his fresh supply of meat and hide to the village. He walked to the long houses made of cedar planks. He distributed meat to members of his family. In front of one building amid warming rays from the rising sun, there sat a young woman called Shell Seeker but usually known just as Shell. Her long, black hair shone in sunlight to the brightness matched by light flashing from her eyes. She was young and beautiful and from an even earlier age had caught the attention of Gray Raven. She also found natural interest in his spiritual along with physical strength.

"You bring what I really need," she said to her visitor as Gray Raven placed the bundles beside her then sat, leaning his back against the building's cedar planks. Shell and Gray Raven could both look out upon the great expanse of water where swells emerged from the mist of time and distance, moved toward shore, became taller, crested then crashed with a great booming sound, giving voice to express power of this wild, untamable sea. "Amazing to think you and I live here, neighbors to the sea and it is alive just like us," she said, happy to know she had Gray

Raven as her friend, along with the sea, forest and mountains. "I feel so happy," she exclaimed, smiling brightly. "You bring hide and meat to me. I so much enjoy your gifts. You don't have to hold a potlatch to give because you give every day. That's what provides you status with me. In our way of life, status comes not through collecting treasures but in giving them away. That's how prestige comes. In such a process, you get your own happiness and, in turn, you give to me."

"You're in a good mood this morning," observed Gray Raven.

"You complete my world," she replied. "Because you bring me supplies, I can make blankets. I have work to do, a place in the sun that is now rising upon a new day. Everyday is precious. Each one only comes once. We can never go back to repeat one or change one part. I notice you greet each new day when you sit by the shore and watch golden rays from the sun add light and color to swells coming always onward, leaving behind the old day and coming to announce the new by standing up, cresting then crashing down in a thundering roar."

"I enjoy hearing your thoughts," said Gray Raven. "Your work too is beautiful. You add twisted, cedar bark to goat hair to make blankets. They are not just pretty ornaments. They hold our traditions. In cedar bark designs, you record Quinault stories past and present. I see and remember your symbols, designs and crests, all expressing our narrative traditions. I have learned these patterns, designs, symbols and crests of our people. All that is cherished in the customs of our past, I have obtained from your blankets."

"You give to me and I give to you," she said. "As I have mentioned, you know in our society we value and give status or position not through accumulating treasure but by giving it away. Only this act makes us rich."

"You are rich," he replied. "You gather, hold and send out a record of our traditions by writing such designs into your blankets. As I've mentioned, they are not just objects but stories, narrative outlines of our ways of seeing and doing things. Learning all this gives me happiness. I enjoy seeing your work and bringing you supplies."

"I need your supplies to tell my stories," she said. "As I mentioned, you give me a place in the sun with work to do, something to give and giving is treasure."

"Your designs and symbols are ways of talking," he observed. "Would you care to go swimming?"

She stood up and they walked to the water. As they waded into the surf, a particularly large swell approached. Sunlight flashed golden hues along this moving, seeming to be a living wall of water. Into cresting, moving life, they both dove. Turbulence swirled above them as the swell tumbled past, rushing onward toward shore. The two swimmers poked their heads through the surface to catch warmth from the sun. Gray Raven was surprised when she clamped onto him. Suddenly warm again, he joined her in a journey beyond where he thought life could go.

Returning to shore, Gray Raven and Shell started walking along the border between dry sand and flows of water sent by each breaking swell. Rays of sunlight brought warmth and golden light to both land and water. Gulls circling overhead added streaks of white to a seemingly endless blue sky. Rocks loomed largely out of the water in addition to lining the shore. Onward the two people walked, moving as two parts together, joining with other life flows as part of one life, breathing in and out.

"You understand this life better than other people," said Shell, to her companion. "You see beyond the way things appear to be and live in the spirit world you say is the only life. Nothing else lives forever."

"You will," he replied. "You seek and believe in the Creator. That's all you have to do to be at home, to get home. We live in the spirit world. We don't stay here long among things like rocks."

"Your words give me happiness," she said.

"Your company and symbols, designs and crests give me happiness," he replied. "Someday, I'd like to work with your symbols and use them to tell a narrative story of our village's traditions."

"Good idea," she replied. "I write our story into blankets. What will you use to record the traditions of our people?"

"If I am able to do so, I'll write our story into copper using both symbols and words. Words of course are symbols."

"I have traveled a long way with you today," she said.

"And I have seen a long way with you," he replied.

"You see more than most people every day," she added, smiling brightly just as sun flashed on a particularly tall swell before it curled then came down in a crashing boom of spraying water. "All days are important. We get them one at a time. If we waste one or spoil something, we can't go back and relive the time. Once passing, the time segment has gone forever, making us one day older. Like sand tumbling from our open hand, each part is counted. When the hand is empty, our life goes and we return to the spirit world we left when we were born here on earth to start another lifetime."

"You have nothing to learn from me," he stated. "You see as far as I do. Each moment I share with you, I wonder why I have to be away so long."

"I have always wondered the same thing about you," she replied. "Maybe we should plan things better. Are the plans for us to make?" she asked.

"At times like this, I think you see more than I can," he said.

"Each day is important," she confirmed.

"That's why I greet each one," he said.

"Maybe we should start back to the village," she suggested. "I live there. I know you live here, at home with the sea, forest and mountains. Today I have lived with you here and I'll never forget you. I have seen your world and could live there but right now I know or feel, I also have a home back at the wooden houses. We'll see what the future brings. This time though, or day, I'll remember. There are those shining moments in life when the spiritual most noticeably touches the physical. We live in the spiritual world although we continue to be on the physical earth. All things for a moment are perfect and happiness does not have to be sought, just enjoyed. Life is present and glows. We see what is/was meant to be."

"If you are ready, we will start back to the village," he said.

"Then you are returning here, aren't you?" she confirmed.

"Yes," he said, "although it'll never be the same again without you being here."

"That's what memory is for," she observed, smiling again.

"Yes," he said, seeing paths dividing ahead of them and not liking the feeling. "We have seized the moment and enjoyed the day. That's the best we can do. Life comes in days. Making the most of each one is trying our best and that's all there is. Generally, I think our trails are established and all we can do is our best each day. We can't jump ahead but I like to see the future."

"I hope you're in mine," she said, smiling again.

"We are both there in some way," he added.

Page

Without noticing distance being walked, they were surprised to see again on the shore ahead the wooden structures of the village.

Night came and Gray Raven slept on the sand. The last sounds he heard at night and first in the morning were the booms of long swells crashing along the shore.

To start the new day, he walked to the form of the great sixty-foot canoe, emerging chip by chip from a long cedar log resting on planks beside the sea. Resuming his skilled craftsmanship, he helped other carvers bring the canoe out of the log. As the other two workers, he could see the craft and there remained only the task of chipping away by fire and adz the extra wood.

When the other workers rested, Gray Raven left to get more goat hides and meat for Shell in addition to acquiring meat for members of his family. Aside from bringing Shell hides and cedar bark for her blankets and supplying meat in addition to other materials for members of his family, he was not seen in the village. Increasingly, his home became the thundering sea, the forest and mountains.

He constantly gathered knowledge of his home in the woods where he walked in awe of trees he knew had been alive for countless years. Through this length of time communities of life had gathered including birds and mammals along with vegetation, such as mosses and vines.

One morning, he sat on the sand, as he usually did, to watch the new day begin. The rising sun gradually brought golden rays to flash upon rollers moving toward shore. Each swell became taller and crested before dropping in a booming explosion of water rushing onward to spread out over sand only to drain back again into the base of the next thundering rush of surging water.

The sea displays power all the time, through day and night, observed Gray Raven. *The sea brings treasures including floating remnants of boats belonging to other shores. On some of these wooden pieces there has been attached what we have come to call float iron. Such metal floats in on sections of* wrecked boats. *I've been using this metal to help with my work. I also like jade and the transparent stone.*

I live with the sea, forests and mountains and they are all alive, mused Gray Raven one morning, while sitting beside his fire on the gravel shore of a river. He had speared a salmon and this fish now roasted on a stick settled above flames. *I like to cook meat for a long time. Extra cooking seems to bring out the true flavor of the food.*

All parts of my surroundings are alive, he thought while observing his region. *Each bird, animal, fish, plant, tree or other aspect of life is different yet there is a common presence flowing through all and this is the spiritual connection of the Creator. Not all people see this unity of life because they don't live here as I do. Looking in from a distance can never replace the understanding of what is home. My home is life itself and I see as companions not just people in my village but all parts with whom we are joined, such as fish, trees, goats, sheep and even the black as well as the much scarcer brown bears. What good is a gift, if we don't*

26

understand it? Someone can give me a piece of float iron; however, what good is it if I don't see its possible usefulness? What good is life if we don't know what it's for? I've always asked such questions and maybe that's why I'm here and others are not. I know life is an opportunity we have asked for to hone our spirits against the rocks of adversity to improve by such methods not available in the spiritual side where there is no trouble. Time has come, he decided, *to savor this food, drink some of the cold, clear, water then soak in the river to become clean both on the outside and inside.*

Gray Raven followed his meal with a drink of water then he stepped into the stream, got down and stretched out in it, resting his back against pebbles while water swirled and splashed across his chest. Occasionally his head became covered by the constantly flowing cold, clear, stream.

The chill tightened his muscles and awakened his mind to clarity he could only reach during such occasions or in emergencies. He was enjoying clarity when a cloud crossed over his new insightfulness.

He stood up, worried. He returned to his fire and added wood until flames ascended to match his height. They brought outside warmth, even heat, yet his spirit felt a chill.

He walked to his cache of weapons and armor. He put on the slats of protective covering, added the wooden helmet and lastly picked up spears in addition to bow and arrows. Ready for trouble, he started returning to the village along one of very few trails used as inland trade routes.

It was not long before he saw them. They walked in a long line, having apparently leaders in front, captives in the middle and others following. With the raid over, men had removed their helmets and armor and tied all items in place to make traveling easier and faster.

Rushing ahead of the enemies, Gray Raven selected the closest place on the trail where large numbers would not be an advantage in a battle because only a single member of the group could fight at one time. This situation was presented on the trail where the route ran between two rock walls. Here only one enemy from this large group could attack Gray Raven at one time. Also, he wore armor and the others had removed such protection.

As the lead raider came through the narrow part on the trail, Gray Raven shot an arrow that stuck in the man's lower chest, sending him sprawling backwards. The next men to rush forward were also dropped by arrows until a few arrows also came toward Gray Raven. One stuck in his shoulder, making the use of his bow impossible. He ran forward and dropped attackers by using his spears. Finally, he swung his club with a fury only a cornered attacker knows.

Having to step past and even climb over fallen comrades, the attackers lost the fire for battle. Leaders were dead. The others decided this battle had been lost and time had come to travel home by a different route, leaving behind the prisoners who had charged up the trail and gone through the narrows.

Gray Raven had given a great gift to his people. Those he had rescued swarmed him, showering him with gratitude for saving their lives. Upon returning to the village, Gray Raven, who had given more than was done in the usual type of potlatch, walked for many days in exalted prestige. Such status was extended to all his family members and so was the high point of happy days marking his first lifetime, the duration of his youth.

The next days, starting his second lifetime, were not as happy. He, as expected, returned to his home with sea, forest and mountains.

Spending additional time in the forest, he started to see more of it as it took him into not a physical world but a spiritual place. *I knew before all these parts, each one unique, work together in harmony of peacefulness and permanence*, he recalled. *Even events appearing to be harsh, such as a wolf or person killing to get food, are part of a larger plan where all events have a purpose. Just people can upset the order because they are the only components who can or will decide to break away and not do what is best in the sacredness of life but what they think will bring them more gain. Such individuals stop believing in the Creator and start traveling according to their own route.*

Walking to a particularly large and tall tree, Gray Raven said to himself, *I'm going to do what so many other creatures and plants establish on this tree as I'm going to build a house. This tree is easy to climb because the branches are close together and there are many vines. I'll construct planks then make nettle fiber cords to pull each piece of split cedar up to my small building.*

He started working, beginning by cutting sections of cedar and splitting them to get planks. *Having a straight grain,* he observed, *red cedar splits evenly when a bone or yew wedge is inserted into the wood and a stone hammer is used to pound the insert to start the split. A jade adz works well to smooth each split piece before it is used to form the shelter.*

At the building site, he fit each plank, making a flat area to serve as a beginning of the small house yet in appearance it could be accepted as being just part of the tree. When the walls went up, openings were left so the outside forest would not be separated from the interior. After the roof was in place the completed structure provided a comfortable home and, above all, it kept out the almost constant rain.

With the tree structure completed, Gray Raven used it for sleeping. He made long boxes to store some of his few tools. Last, he added benches so he could sit to rest while watching the top part of the forest, mainly the realm of birds.

Sitting on a just completed bench, he looked out at the branches and foliage and decided, *I must build an actual platform for sleeping. I'll likely always have to climb up the tree by using branches as steps. Yet if I protect my hands with shredded and twisted cedar bark, I could slide down on vines or cords made of twisted fiber. I'll continue to do all cooking on the pebble bank of the river. Along with the shelter I've made there, I now have two places for sleeping.*

Gray Raven kept returning to high places to get goat hides and meat for Shell. In one region, he did not have to climb beyond where clouds moved because goats descended half way to get water from a pool formed from a small flow trickling down a rock wall. The goats found footing along this same wall and descended to drink deeply.

Occasionally, Gray Raven met the animals at this watering place or he waited motionlessly like a rock himself until the goats arrived. They returned to lofty heights, leaving a ram next to the pool.

Gray Raven was taking a hide and meat to Shell when he wondered if he was in his own village. Everything felt different although most people and places appeared to be the same. There just seemed to be a gray film between it and him.

The spell partially broke when he approached Shell and she said, "You bring sunlight to my day when you visit me."

"You are the only sunlight I see in this village," he replied. "Has something changed or am I just imagining things? Maybe I've just been away too long."

"You have been away too long," she confirmed.

"I didn't think I'd be so missed," he said.

"You were missed always by me and your family but this time by the whole village," she explained. "When you were away, there was another raid against the village. This time enemies came from the water by canoe as attackers usually come and not by trade routes across land where you met them during the previous occasion. The people missed you by your absence. When you were needed, you did not give them your help. Prestige comes, as you know, by what you can give. The people now judge you because of your extended times of absence, as not contributing to the community anymore. You, and your family along with you, have lost importance. How you will ever fix this, I don't know. You could say you are in a second lifetime, leaving happiness behind and enduring days of disfavor. You have also hurt me."

Shock gripped him. The news clouded his view. Previous grayness suddenly had a cool edge to it.

"I would never normally say this but I thought I would marry you and I will always feel this way and think of you as my husband," she said, with paleness appearing in her eyes. "That's my choice and the way I will be. My family is no longer considering you because of your fall from importance and has arranged for me to marry a man who has prestige in the village. Such is the way people think so that's how my life is. What has happened to your life? The sea, forest and mountains took you to themselves. This village no longer considers you a person of high standing. I will always have some sadness now but, unlike you, I live here."

"How can I change such a situation and take away this dark cloud?" he asked.

"I don't know," she replied. "I trust you and think you will find a way. Thank you for bringing goat hair for my blankets. I will pretend that life goes on."

"I will have to fix this predicament," he whispered before he turned and walked back to his tree house. He remained there for some days and nights until he knew he had to climb down and get food or he would not leave the house again.

After stepping from one branch to another until reaching the ground, he left the tree and walked to the river shelter to get salmon for food and begin carving a small canoe. *I'll use it,* he decided, *to start collecting sea otter furs in demand by American and English traders, arriving by ships along the coast.*

My home is the sea, forest and mountains. I can find, in my home, a sufficient number of sea otters to exchange for copper that the people are calling coppers. They are the most prized items in our village used to achieve status and prestige. I do not seek high position but have been looking for a good substance I can use to record all the wondrous customs, stories and traditions of the Quinault people. I'll apply the symbols, designs, emblems and crests Shell has taught me as she weaves them into her blankets. In copper, I'll carve the great narrative stories of our people. I'll record our life. I know of copper outcroppings that have been eroded into view along riverbanks. There is also copper in the wall of the cave I located by watching the great, brown bear. I was watching when the forest giant walked to the edge of the cliff, held up one paw then raked it down through air, as if marking a stump, establishing his territory. A slight breeze, coming upward from the river valley, rippled fur along bear's rugged sides. The creature, standing, gazed out at the world and turned his head slowly in a half circle, looking everywhere without fear. The bear uses the cave to sleep through the winter. I'm there at other times and can collect copper, pounding it into shape. I'll do the same from copper protruding from riverbanks. I'll add this supply to sheets, plates or other panels I can get from traders. Shield-shaped forms and panels of hammered copper, in addition to sheets or plates will hold stories I'll tell by carving.

In our ways of living, leaders are people who obtain status not through acquiring wealth but by giving it away, usually in a formalized celebration of the potlatch, a word that means giving. I don't seek status but when my people see my narrative records in copper, a most prized item among our people, I along with my family will receive again high status. This time will be my third lifetime.

Staying at the riverside shelter, Gray Raven started carving a small canoe. He started, as always, with the process of cutting a cedar log. He built a fire at the tree's base then chipped the burned wood away using an adz with a jade blade. After the tree fell into the water, he removed unwanted branches by using a cutting adz of transparent stone. He also had an iron bladed adz. He got this metal from float iron. It drifted to shore from wrecks out at sea.

He floated the trunk to a stand he had made next to the river. Fiber ropes helped fit the log into place. He removed unwanted wood by burning it then chipping to unwrap the canoe and free it from outside layers.

While working on the canoe, he lived at his riverside shelter. Each day was much the same as those that came before. An indication of time passing was the gradual emergence of the canoe from the log.

The canoe was not the only progress made at the river camp. Much earlier, while burning and chipping, he, as usual, felt companionship of his surroundings and his spiritual oneness with them. Something else though was added early one morning before sunrays warmed the canoe site. Gray Raven realized he was being watched. The curious onlooker was a coyote pup. The eyes were yellow and fur coloring blended from white through gray to black. "I'm going to call you Smoke," said Gray Raven to the watcher.

At the sound of the words the pup's tail wagged slightly and Gray Raven said, "A bond has been made. I have a new friend."

As days passed, visits increased and Gray Raven started to supply small pieces of meat. Smoke was the only one to enter the camp. Although not approaching as closely, other pups occasionally came into view along with two adult coyotes.

When the coyote was almost full size, he visited alone and received larger pieces of meat. The canoe gradually was freed from the log and helped Gray Raven to acquire sea otter furs. They were used to get copper plates and sheets from the traders.

After acquiring sufficient coppers from the visitors arriving by ship along the coast, Gray Raven started removing copper from riverbanks. He also dislodged large sections from walls at the cave. All coppers were kept in the cave.

He heated copper, particularly larger pieces and pounded the forms into usable shapes. Following much work, he acquired the quantity of copper he sought as time passed during what he considered to be his second lifetime, a period when he had fallen into disfavor at his village and he was, as seen by others, except Shell and his family, an outcast, one who did not give when giving was needed and as a result he lost status.

In the cave, he assembled along ledges his coppers. There were panels and shield-shaped sections of hammered forms. On these he marked crests, symbols, designs and emblems of the Quinault people. Using plates and sheets of copper obtained from traders, he carved narrative history telling the story and traditions of the Quinault nation. Each copper he signed with a sign or English words he was learning.

Before starting the main part of telling the story and traditions in copper, Gray Raven rested. During his first morning of rest he awoke early as he usually did. In first light of dawn, he kindled a small fire outside the cave in the fire pit he always used. Prepared as a special celebration, he skewered some pieces of sheep meat. Next, in a pot set at the edge of the fire, he had added water along with crushed coffee beans. *Coppers are not the only things I have traded from the Americans and English who come to these shores,* he thought. *The pots are useful along with frying pan and iron chisel. Mainly though, I now enjoy starting each day with a mug of coffee. As long as the traders bring coffee, I'll be out in my canoe to greet them. Maybe I could grow coffee. I'm not the only one to acquire new tastes. My coyote friend, Smoke, now prefers meat to be cooked.* Gray Raven and Smoke had both started to greet the new day before first rays of sunlight cast golden outlines across the outside of the cave, where the two friends sat.

Each day, when the coyote arrived, Gray Raven greeted him with a few pieces of cooked meat. Next they both sat away from the fire where skewered meat sizzled above flames. Smoke, after finishing his meal along with water, sat and watched the valley below. Beside him, Gray Raven rested while sipping a second mug of black, strong coffee. Below them, mist or thin clouds moved, occasionally blocking the view and turning to golden strands in the new sunlight. Beyond such mist, there was a wide golden path of the river. This morning a line of elk crossed the stream.

To the coyote, Gray Raven said, "When the people of my village receive my coppers, I will start my third lifetime. Copper is one of the most prized possessions of our people. Through such gifts, actually my celebration of a potlatch, I'll achieve prestige and high standing. Most importantly, others will stop opposing us. Shell and I will get married."

Turning to look more closely at his companion, Gray Raven said, "You don't need coppers to get your mate. I see she often travels with you but stays back as you enter this camp. When I see you getting up to leave, I'll give you extra pieces of meat so she can take part in our feasts."

Continuing to work with the coppers, Gray Raven told the story of the Quinault nation. Before he worked on a copper, he placed each one in front of coals of a fire to provide warmth that seemed to enable deeper carving in slightly softer material and thereby stop small cracks from appearing.

To mark the copper he used iron chisels along with wooden handled carving tools also tipped with iron or sharply polished transparent stone. Wooden hammers applied the right amount of force. They effectively pounded lines into the material less deeply than hammers of stone.

The type of copper determined the story it could tell. Large, heaviest pieces were the panels of hammered copper in addition to those pounded into the shape of shields. To each of these pieces, he tapped in crests, designs, emblems and other symbols. They were copies of long cherished traditions. For such sections, he used chisels tapped by wooden hammers. Slowly, having awareness of the importance of detail, he brought to life in copper, great records of accomplishments.

Requiring less repetition of long held patterns and emblems, the telling of narrative traditions was a particularly fascinating process of writing into the metal. He used old symbols along with letters he had learned from the English language. Always in symbols or letters he marked his name on each completed section.

When his great achievements were completed, he again rested. After the first meal of the next day including meat shared with Smoke, both man and coyote sat in front of remnants of the fire while they watched the valley below. Ravens flew past, lower in height than the two watchers. The birds' wings could be heard brushing against moist, morning air. Sunrays gradually cleared mist. Again the river below turned to a trail of gold winding between pebbled shores.

"When the people see what I have accomplished with these works, holding narrative histories and designs, I will be restored to a position of prestige," said Gray Raven to his companion who communicated without words but by a seemingly unlimited range of looks and glances. The sound of today's words brought contentment. "I will be restored to a status of importance and leadership. There are few items in our community cherished as much as objects of copper. I have prepared not just objects but records of our traditions and ways of life. When I acquire a new position of high standing, all opposition will vanish to the marriage of Shell and me."

Gray Raven and Smoke left the cave and walked down to the forest. Smoke naturally knew the forest's life. After years of learning or remembering,

Gray Raven also traveled in company with all connecting aspects of life, such as trees, plants, mosses, animals and birds. Seeing, feeling, and comforted by all these companions, Gray Raven, along with his friend walked to the coast.

As usual, there was power in display here varied yet similar to the strength of forests and mountains. *Spiritual presence*, observed Gray Raven, *connects each part of wilderness and shows power. This force roars when each advancing swell stands up, gets caught in sunlight and blazes with gold just before crashing down in a display of strength to shake the shore.*

Gray Raven and his companion sat. They watched the restless sea as two rocks among so many others. *If anyone thinks,* reflected Gray Raven, *that there is no sacred presence connecting each part of Creation, I would want to ask them how they would explain my companion has four legs and gray fur but is my friend? We have differences but much more in common, connecting us.*

When Smoke was absent, traveling with his mate, Gray Raven used such intervals to get goat fur and meat for Shell. He often climbed different routes to not disturb the same goats too often.

During a new day, before sunlight cleared away mist or moving clouds, Gray Raven followed a new route. He climbed until he was above ravens calling and frolicking below. He was not higher than an eagle that watched him with yellow eyes as the majestic bird flew past.

Near a place where rams assembled, Gray Raven stopped and nocked an arrow to his yew bow. Akin to a gust of wind, the rams filled the clearing. One of them fell with an arrow protruding from its side.

Gray Raven worked with skilled and swift strokes, saving meat and using the hide as a carrying pack. The downward walk started, bringing Gray Raven into a thick, moving cloud. It obscured the trail.

I've come too far down to go back, he thought. *I can't stop on this ledge. I must proceed. I can rest after I get back to camp. I have to continue, although I've picked up an unwelcome companion. It is worry. I dislike stepping into a moving cloud. It hides danger and thereby increases it. I don't think I'm feeling fear but I'm too smart not to worry about this terrible situation I'm in; I can't stop or go back. Therefore proceeding is all I can do.*

He stepped on a rock and it slid toward the edge of the cliff. *I have to lift my foot off this loose rock although I can't see the next step. I must hit solid terrain if I move toward the wall.*

The next step sent his foot sliding into the cloud. For an instant, he knew he was in the cloud, caught in a wind tunnel. A light flashed. Among those of the spiritual world approaching him, his white dog was in the lead, rushing ahead of Gray Raven's family members and friends. Waiting in the distance was Shell.

Chapter 2

The Three Lives of Raylon James

Present Day

Pelicans soared past as expected at the completion of another perfect day along the shore of Florida facing the Gulf of Mexico. The sun, by approaching the horizon, took much brightness out of light, making more apparent colors already present and increasing them because of haze above the water. Red hues topped the others, painting both sky and water. Waves rolling toward shore were etched by red outlines while cresting before breaking and crashing into turbulence sending sheets of water over sand only to be withdrawn again and replaced by the next flow. Sandpipers searched the flows, hunting for food, particularly coquinas.

Raylon James finished putting away his fishing equipment after throwing the last of the scaled sardines, known generally as greenbacks, to his fishing companions, the heron and egret. Full again, the birds spread their wings, displaying majestic arrays of feathers and climbed the red sky to prepare for the night.

Raylon sat on his folding chair, next to his neatly packed equipment and might appear to any of the people walking past to be a man as any other except he was fishing from the beach in front of a house on top of the ridge beyond the sand. His hair was black although graying. Much like the color of the water, his eyes were greenish blue. Deepening tan helped to disguise his tendency toward being overweight.

If all my life is as easy as my first life, I'll be very lucky, he reflected. *I wonder though, if this evening, with its deepening red sky along with a similar sheen on the water is a warning or just a sign of change to come. My first lifetime has been actually fun, more as the life of a person on vacation. I did not have to seek friends because they came to me. I was seen as being strong and a natural leader, good looking enough to attract women. My present girlfriend, Mylee Clandon, was attracted to me when we were young and now we are partners with lots of friends. High marks from courses came almost without much effort and I've graduated sufficient times to be well qualified for employment of my choice. Money our family retains and I have, too. Employment I've always had but money coming in from secure investments is much greater than wages. I've had cars of my choice, in addition to this house in Florida.*

But I feel the red sky and water are warnings. Will clouds enter my clear sky? My girlfriend and I have sort of been together since we were kids. She always seemed to come to see me and I am pleased she did. My first job was working as a ranger in the office of the Forest Service, Beaverhead Mountains of the Bitterroot Range. The Lewis and Clark

51

Expedition went through Lemi Pass on Lolo Trail in August 1805. They were leaving behind the headwaters of the Missouri River and entering headwaters of the Columbia River. They crossed this area on foot and got good horses from the Shoshoni. The Shoshoni Chief, Cameahwait, turned out to be the brother of Sacajawea who was helping to guide the expedition. She had been captured when twelve years old and taken eastward by the Hidatsa. A trader-trapper, Charbonneau, married her. Lewis and Clark hired Charbonneau to get the guiding knowledge of Sacajawea. My interest in that story lies in the fact there was no bond between Sacajawea and her so-called husband but there was one between Sacajawea and Captain Clark.

"Any time you're ready," shouted Mylee from the top of the hill at the back of the beach and in front of the house.

"OK," he called in reply. Looking again at the water, he saw backs of porpoises breaking from the red sea then submerging, leaving behind a panorama where colors were deepening to purple.

I've had an easy first lifetime, he though again. *I've seen many red sunsets. They usually turn red during the latter part of a day. Why should I wonder if this purple sky and red sea are a warning or an omen?*

He walked up the steps to his house, went inside and was struck by the beauty of Mylee. With dark blonde hair dropping to her shoulders outlining fine features and deep blue eyes, she was slim and now wearing a white dress. "When you are ready, we are both ready," she said.

Raylon put away his fishing equipment, showered, donned clean clothes and was prepared to leave in time to wait for Mylee. He sat on his favorite chair, providing a view of much of a wide room with a gas fireplace bordered by windows on each side. Through these windows, he could be see the last of the red sky as it faded to usher in the night.

"Should we just stay here and order takeout?" he asked Mylee, who was putting dishes away in the kitchen.

"Maybe after a brief visit to the restaurant, we can look forward to coming back here," she replied. "I'm ready now."

"OK," he agreed, getting up off his chair and following her outside to the car. She walked to the driver's door so Ray went around to the passenger's side.

Without talking, they proceeded to their favorite restaurant. Air conditioner supplying cool air together with windows being open tangled currents of coolness in a rush of moist, flower-scented, outside air. Along with the fragrance of flower perfume, there were always present traces of salt and fish.

Leaving the car on the lot, Mylee gave Ray the keys, saying, "Maybe you would want to drive back. These are your keys. Mine are at home."

Mylee led the way to the restaurant, stepping into a vast building with a main section of buffet counters joined by rooms with tables and chairs. She walked to her favorite room and table then sat while Ray took his usual place across from her. Almost immediately, servers arrived; Mylee ordered a margarita and Ray, his usual draft beer.

"Maybe we should get started," offered Mylee before she stood up and walked to the buffet followed by Ray. They returned to the table carrying plates topped by an assortment of foods, particularly salmon.

They had just started tasting the meal when another chair at their table was pulled out and a hard looking man sat. He had short, uncombed hair above a well-tanned face with gray eyes and a shadowy beard. A few scars were remnants of a rough life.

"I've seen you here before and thought I should come and visit," he said. "And Ray, you're probably struggling to remember me. I'm Cal Hooper. We were rangers, just starting out with the Forest Service."

"Yes," said Ray. "Our first job was cleaning the kitchen before the cook arrived. We took apart the stoves. We scrubbed each part before putting everything back. When we were finished the room was damp and smelled of soap."

"You later went into accounting and I learned to be a cook," he said. "I've been working on the boats. I invested money and bought an oyster bar down the beach."

"What's the most unusual part of being a cook for a ranger camp?" Mylee asked.

"When most people go out for dinner, the trip is treated as a social event, a time to joke around and swap stories," answered Cal. "Not the same in the ranger camps. There talking is not allowed. At first, this is an adjustment to make but when a person gets used to the custom, it's a habit hard to break. There's no talking so as to have people finish the meal then get out of the way so the cook can clean up and complete the day. Ray and I got started at a camp near the Locksa River, a Nez Perce word meaning rough water. That area has plenty of Lewis and Clark history."

"You have a lot of friends from your ranger days?" Mylee asked Raylon.

Answering for him, Cal said, "You meet and work with people all through life but very few of them are actually friends."

"I would agree with that assessment," added Ray.

"I would too," observed Mylee. "Are you here with a girlfriend?" she asked Cal.

"They all seem to be much the same, sort of," he answered. "I meet a lot of them. Almost never do I meet one I'd like to keep. If such a sight occurs, I can be ruthless because I want to have some fun."

Standing, Cal said, "I'd better let you enjoy the meal."

After he had walked away, Mylee said, "That was a character, from your past."

"A long time ago," added Ray.

Raylon finished one draft, put his glass down and said, "Have to go for a walk to the washroom."

He entered the washroom. When he was leaving, Cal's form filled the doorway and he said, "We worked together a long time ago and as I hinted at your table, we were not friends. I still don't enjoy doing this but you've got what I want."

Almost before the words ended, Cal grabbed Ray and slammed him against a wall, stunning him. A flashing right fist then a left knocked Ray out. Cal half supported and partly carried him out a side door then left him sprawled on the ground behind some garbage bins.

Walking back to the table where Mylee remained, Cal explained, "Ray got sick on the food and had to leave. He asked me to give you a ride home. I have a truck parked on the back lot. When you're ready, I'll give you a ride."

"I'm going to see if he's all right," she stated.

"He has gone—left," countered Cal. "He's only sick because of something he ate. He's OK. He told me he wanted you to have a good evening and you're not to worry about him."

"He'd say that regardless of what shape he was in," she said.

"On the way home, could I show you my restaurant?" he asked.

"You certain Ray is OK?" she pushed.

"He said he's fine—just an upset stomach and nothing to get in the way of you enjoying the outing," explained Cal.

"If you're certain Ray's not hurt, it would be interesting to see your restaurant," she agreed.

"He said not to worry because he was all right and he wanted to be sure you were OK," said Cal, after getting the server to bring refills to the drinks. When they arrived he said, "That'll help you relax."

Next morning, at the back of the restaurant, a falling trash can lid caused Ray to open his eyes. He heard the varying calls of a mocking bird announce the arrival of first light brightening a new day. Another clanking sound brought Ray's attention to raccoons raiding the restaurant's garbage pails. "Inside there's one buffet and outside there's another," said Ray to a large raccoon crunching on remnants of last night's special while staring directly at Ray. "You guys are related to bears and you have similar dining habits," continued Ray. "I'm pleased I'm meeting the smaller members of the family here this morning and, in case some of you were asking with that chatter of yours, my head aches."

Raylon stood up, making his head throb as if a freight train was rumbling past the garbage pails. Searching his pockets, he found nothing had been taken except cash. He walked to the front of the building and was pleased to see his car. He drove to his house. It stood in first golden rays of sunlight breaking from the east and bringing what at least appeared to be just another day as the others.

I almost expected, thought Ray after he parked his car and walked to the house, *there would be some change to the surroundings because my life has changed. Pelicans are soaring above waves as they always do each day and porpoises are swimming past, their backs occasionally breaking through the surface. New hibiscus flowers are starting to open up. Each one lasts for only one day; but my life has changed.*

Unlocking the door and stepping inside his house, he checked the phone for messages, hoping to hear from Mylee and she had left a message, "Cal convinced me you were all right. I'm starting an interesting job serving at Cal's Blue Heron Oyster Bar and will be delayed getting home. I hope this sits well with you but I think you and I have the same attitude of exploring life to see what it offers and not just follow any path but discover what is available then select what's best for us."

Chapter 3

The Second Life of Raylon James

Sitting, Ray thought, *my first lifetime was easy—and fun. I'm starting now my second lifetime, an occasion when I have to get stronger. Because I'm not strong enough, I don't want to ever again get slammed up against a washroom wall and left outside with the garbage. The advantage I can take from my easy time in life will be a financial base from which to operate.*

After preparing breakfast of a toasted, fried egg sandwich, he sat down again on his favorite chair, which provided a view of the Gulf, where normally, he would be sitting by the shore and fishing accompanied by the heron and egret. *I have to start fishing for a different goal and that is my increased strength,* he determined. *To carry out this objective, I think I'll now explore what I've always considered doing and that is visiting the national parks. I'll gather as much information as I can collect in a short time and also start purchasing camping equipment of all kinds.*

Starting the next day, Ray entered what was, for him, a new world. With guidance from numerous knowledgeable people, he purchased what he thought was all the equipment he could possibly require including tent, cook stove and special clothing. He also checked the parks until there was only one that met what he needed and that was Olympic National Park in the northwestern corner of Washington State.

I know, he declared in his mind, *I've found the park to meet my current dreams because Olympic National Park is listed as being ninety-five percent wilderness and much of that is old growth forest. Of further interest, the park has three different regions with Pacific coast, temperate rain forest and mountains. I could also step away from the park boundaries to reach similar country without intruding on other people. This place calls to me in my time of need.*

The night before departure, Raylon was gripped by a worried feeling he could not shake, for it had gradually overtaken his life. As he tossed without sleeping, he reasoned, *I have caught the premonition I'm late for something and must hurry even when there seems to be no particular reason for rushing.*

While a mockingbird sang in the darkness before dawn, Ray placed a large cup of coffee in the holder that was part of the car's armrest, opened a box of muffins and, accompanied by these items, his journey started.

With windows open, he let the morning freshness come inside his packed vehicle. He noticed an opossum that had just finished drinking from a pool of water formed at the roadside after rain during the night. *Always liked opossums,* thought Ray before he threw this resident a muffin. *Opossums are related to kangaroos and carry their young in a pouch. Opossums help people by eating many ticks.*

My second lifetime begins with this journey, Ray reflected, *and I'm ready for such a new phase. It seems to have been prearranged as our lives are set in broad strokes and we only have to make decisions along the way, determining our progress. Amazing to consider, if life is forever, we live spiritually in the spirit world or heaven and come to earth maybe many times and plan out the rough outlines of each visit before we come here to learn in earth's school of hard knocks how to improve in ways not available in heaven where there is no trouble. My life is similar to the opossum's. We are both connected by the Creator; but as a person, I have the dilemma of having to think things over to a greater extent. Some people decide to turn against the Creator, turn their backs and go their own way, thereby making their own hell, something the Creator would never do. Opossums are lucky because they don't have a choice to turn or not turn against the Creator. They will be in the spirit world and meet us there when we return.*

I'd better pay attention to where I'm going, Ray warned himself. *I enjoy the warmth of Florida along with the freshness or moisture in the air with a scent of flowers, foliage, salt and fish.*

Stopping at Fort Walton Beach, he was amazed by the white, sugar-like sand in addition to clear water. Before leaving Florida, he stopped at a waterfront restaurant and ordered his favorite grouper sandwich with cheese accompanied by a glass of orange juice along with a slice of fresh and delicious key lime pie.

Traveling again, he did some gambling at a casino in Mississippi then rented a room for one night at a hotel in New Orleans. While there he walked along Bourbon Street and stopped at a restaurant that had foods mentioned in Hank William's song Jambalaya such as crayfish pie and file gumbo. In the background, by recorded music, Randy Lewis was singing "Roll on Mississippi".

Next morning, pleased to be traveling again, starting with a cup of coffee and a fresh new day,

Page

Ray marveled at the extent of the watery region the highway crossed over along the way to Galveston, Texas. He rented a room at a waterfront motel. Following a fine meal at the adjoining restaurant, he walked the beach at low tide on the waterside of the sea wall. Pink barnacles decorated the wall as roses and other debris, likely dumped from a passing cruise ship, littered much of the sand.

That evening, Ray sat out on the motel's deck and watched waves bring to shore a shrimp boat. A man jumped from the boat before the vessel returned to deeper water. The discharged crewmember walked up to Ray and explained, "I had an argument with the captain so he dumped me here. Could you give me some cash to help me get a bus ticket to return home?"

Ray generously helped the fellow who then left and night arrived. The morning started with a box of muffins and a tall cup of takeout coffee from the restaurant.

Traveling northwestward through Texas, Ray came to much dry and arid country where an important crop was cotton. A sign next to a side road reported, "Home of Judge Roy Bean". *I won't go in there,* thought Ray, *because the man had a reputation as the hanging judge. He seemed to find hanging to be the best sentence for most people he judged.*

When Ray later mentioned Roy Bean at a gas and coffee shop, the fellow behind the counter said, "Judge Roy Bean took the law into his own hands."

"During earlier times in Texas," recalled Ray, "a man could get hung for stealing a horse."

The fellow behind the counter said, "Texas never had a horse that needed stealing but Texas had a lot o' men who needed hanging."

Returning to the highway, Ray drove through an ice storm while crossing the Llano Estacado, the Staked Plain. At night he rented a room at a ranch style motel with a restaurant where there was no menu but only a choice. A person could have grilled pork or beef with a side of beans.

Enjoying the meal, Ray thought, *that's as delicious as beef and beans get. The singers here called The Ranch Hands are as outstanding as the food.*

In the first light of dawn next morning, Ray was sipping coffee while driving across the border into Arizona. At Bowie, he turned off the interstate, drove past a stand of pistachio trees then went through Apache Pass near Fort Bowie, leading to the Chiricahua Mountains. He stopped in Tombstone where there had been a gunfight at the still present O K Corral. The shooting was between the Clantons and Earps, including the dentist, John Henry Holliday, generally known as Doc Holliday.

After parking his car, Ray starting a walking tour. Entering the Bird Cage Theatre, he thought, *the reputation of this place is many times larger than the actual size of the theater.*

Outside again, stepping into a dry, hot sunlit day, Ray moved on to the Boothill Graveyard where there was displayed more poetry than sentiment, such as George Johnson who unknowingly bought a horse from the guy who stole it and as a result got hung by the other good citizens who put on his marker, "Here Lies George Johnson Hanged by Mistake 1882 He Was Right We was Wrong But We Strung Him Up And Now He's Gone".

Ray continued his tour of historic shops where there were many horseshoes for sale. Many people were preparing for a fast draw contest. Ray heard one guy say to another, "Competition's going to be tough this year. I just noticed a license plate from Florida."

Traveling northward in Arizona, Ray stopped to visit some ruins left by the Anasazi people. By checking information about them he discovered Anasazi is a Navaho word meaning Ancient Ones. They had many settlements in the southwest yet they experienced a drought in the 1400s then moved northward to get water. The Anasazi today are known as the Hopi, Zuni, and Pueblo. More recently arrived people are the Navaho who today occupy areas covering Anasazi ruins, such as Canyon de Chelly. *I'll stop for the night*, decided Ray, *in the Navaho community at the Cameron Trading Post that includes a motel, gift shop and restaurant.*

The motel room was expansive and furnished with Southwestern scenes of the nearby Little Colorado River. Along its banks, sheep and horses grazed.

The restaurant was also unmistakably Southwestern with log furnishings and scenes of horses grazing on vast plains. The woman bringing the glass of draft had long, black hair bordering her beautiful face where her eyes, when caught in rays of sunlight shining through numerous windows, where revealed to be not black but brown.

After checking the menu, Ray requested the Navajo taco, a local favorite. *I notice,* observed Ray, *that around here they spell Navaho as Navajo.*

Taking the order, the woman said, "You won't be disappointed by the taco. That really is a favorite."

Having enjoyed the specialty and ordering another draft, Ray thought, *if more people knew about this fantastic taco, it would be not just a local but a world favorite.*

Light from the rising sun next morning flashed onto Ray after he had driven to the Grand Canyon and now, in this new light, he looked over the edge down to the Colorado River. The drop was of such a distance the air, through its depth, had a presence to it, forming substance. *It's akin to looking out the window of an airplane,* thought Ray. He purchased more coffee along with donuts and enjoyed these treats while driving to Las Vegas, Nevada where he rented a room at a Casino.

After enjoying a meal at the restaurant, he tried a few slot machines, mainly losing. *Like most businesses,* thought Ray, *a casino is profit oriented. It is profitable for customers to see any big wins that happen so such occurrences would take place where most people could see them, such as at corners or other conspicuous sites. Also people who work here would have good advice.*

Seeing an attractive employee who had long, dark hair and black eyes that seemed to often have him in their view, Ray asked her, "Could you suggest a machine that is ready to pay?"

"Try the corner machine by the front door," she suggested.

Strike two, thought Ray. *One more and I'll have a winner.*

"Thank you," he said to the woman. "If the machine agrees with you, I'll share the proceeds."

"I'll be here," she said. "My name is Kim."

Ray sat down at the recommended corner machine near the front door and his losing streak remained loyal to him.

He received beer from a woman carrying a tray of drinks. After enjoying this treat, he stayed with the possibility of a win until the machine signaled to him along with all those nearby and entering the casino that he had won a jackpot. Upon receiving a paper valued at a thousand dollars, he took the winnings to a counter and asked the woman to divide the winnings into two separate piles.

"Thank you," he said before he gave her fifty from each pile. Carrying both bundles, he walked through the casino and finally had to ask if anyone knew where he could find Kim.

"Front door," a man said. "She is just leaving."

Rushing to the front of the casino, Ray saw Kim who had shed her uniform making her part of the casino. She was again just a very attractive woman.

"This is your share," explained Ray, giving her the cash. "I won a thousand minus one hundred for the person who was cashing out winning slips."

"Well this is unusual," she exclaimed after receiving the cash. "Maybe I should do something unusual and take you where I was going."

"If you insist," he replied, starting to walk with her to a car on a nearby lot. She drove him to a house overlooking a desert landscape grotesquely patterned by Joshua trees.

"A Joshua tree is actually a yucca cactus," noted Kim, before she unlocked the door of her house and they both entered. The interior was similar to the outside desert with muted colors conveying a visual impression of permanence. Pictures on walls portrayed sheep and goats.

Seeing him noting the pictures of grazing animals, she said, "I used to raise them. Wild sheep and goats are part of this land."

"You don't have to thank me for sharing the winnings," he said. "You've earned your share."

"Because you're the person who says that, I thank you," she replied. "I give similar advice to people every day at work and you are the first one to share the results. I had also noticed you before we won. On the grill there is goat. Also today there are beans. Does the menu suit you?"

"Perfect selection," he answered, starting to relax for the first time since being slammed up against a washroom wall then waking up with a group of raccoons at the back of the restaurant.

"Beer?" she asked.

"Yes, please," he said.

She brought him a tall, draft glass filled to the rim then she sat down next to him on a sofa. Outside the window, a hawk soared across a seemingly endless azure sky.

"I like the desert," she said. "It's dry and warm. I come from Washington State. It was too cold and too wet."

"I'm going there," he said. "Specifically, I'm traveling to Olympic National Park."

"Yeah," she shouted. "In a small way, you're already there. Most southerners are escapees from the north. I was a ranger at Olympic National Park. I could tell you anything you might want to know about the park."

"That's my destination," he repeated. "Better to know the place before I get there. Please clear away my lack o' knowledge and shine a light on my destination."

"More than ninety-five percent of the park is natural wilderness and much of that is old growth forest," she said, before sipping her margarita.

"You've picked a good place to start," he noted, "because that part is what attracted me to this park and made it stand out among all the others."

"Sip some beer," she said, smiling.

After he enjoyed more of the draft, she continued, "You're going to need some refreshments because I like to talk about two things I know. They are the casino and Olympic National Park.

In 1897, President Grover Cleveland designated the area as Olympic Forest Reserve. President Teddy Roosevelt, in 1909, established Mount Olympic National Monument. In 1938, President Franklin Roosevelt signed an act forming Olympic National Park. The Pacific coast area was added in 1953.

Covering nearly one million acres, actually 922,651 acres, the park includes three different regions. They are Pacific coast, old growth temperate rain forest and mountains. Eleven large river systems draining from Olympic National Park support more than eleven hundred species of plants. The area's four thousand miles of rivers and streams along with eight hundred lakes are a resource for salmon, trout and char that are all part of the salmon family. Inside the park, there are six hundred miles of trails and seventy-five miles of coastline. The region gets from twelve to seventeen feet of rain a year. In 1976 Olympic National Park received the designation of

International Biosphere Reserve and declared a World Heritage Site in 1981."

Noticing that Ray had finished the draft, Kim enjoyed the last of the margarita then stood and walked to the kitchen. She returned quickly to refill the glasses.

"Grill is ready if you want to come outside," she said.

Carrying their glasses, they left the building and Kim said, "You might try the picnic table. I'll bring your grilled goat along with some beans."

"Great restaurant," he exclaimed. "Thank you."

He sat at the table where Kim first put down paper plates. She topped them with large chunks of grilled meat before bringing paper bowls filled with beans. Kim suggested Ray start with the food while she worked to close up the grill then she sat down across from him just as a road runner, at surprising speed, ran beside the table.

"Wonder if road runners are always chased by coyotes out here as happens in cartoons," observed Ray.

"Real life inspires a lot of stories," answered Kim.

"This meat is even more delicious than a meal I enjoyed at a grill in Texas," noted Ray.

"Meat has been grilled on this land since people have been here and that is over twenty thousand years," noted Kim. "If we read some history books we might think the human story on this land only started a number of hundred years ago when the Europeans arrived."

"After over twenty thousand years of experience, the art of grilling food has been perfected," declared Ray.

"You are as generous with compliments as you are at giving away cash," said Kim.

"I was watching the Flintstones program a long time ago," noted Ray, "and Fred Flintstone said, 'Nice guys finish last'. At the time I heard that remark as a warning and recently the omen came true. My first lifetime of an easy life ended when I got slammed up against a washroom wall then woke up among raccoons raiding garbage cans at the back of a restaurant. I realized to face the obstacles in this life, I had to get tougher. So for my second lifetime I'm going to Olympic National Park to find more strength."

"Good idea," said Kim. "I'm getting refills for our glasses because I'm having a great time," she declared before leaving. Returning quickly, she filled the glasses then they both sat back to watch the late evening sun approach the horizon.

Later, in golden haze, the sun sank from view, causing coyotes to call to the approaching night. "The desert is wild and so is Olympic National Park," said Kim. "That's my connection to this place and to you. You're not tame either and that's what I saw in you in the first place. Washroom walls and raccoons are wrong about you. You are strong. You just don't know it yet. I think I know who you are and someday I hope you meet you. I'm celebrating and it's time we pretend to be going in to enjoy some sleep."

"Is this the western hospitality I've heard about?" he asked while they approached an expansive bedroom with windows facing the desert.

"This is better," she answered. "Much, much better."

Next morning, Raylon James opened his eyes and caught the first rays of sunlight flashing from the east and entering windows. Wondering where he was, he looked at his side and saw Kim Brand then he remembered.

He walked to the washroom and started the new day with a shower. Afterward he was pleased to notice the fragrance of perking coffee drifting in the air.

Walking to the kitchen, he found Kim preparing breakfast. "What's on the menu this morning?" he asked.

"Fried eggs and potatoes accompanied by coffee," she answered.

"Can I help?" he asked.

"Yes," she said. "You can sit down at the table, receive breakfast and say it's delicious."

"I like your restaurant," he said, sitting down. "Staff members are friendly."

"The staff members aren't generally as friendly to others as they are to you and they know you are more than you think you are," she replied.

"You are helping me get some of the confidence I needed," he said, after receiving a plate topped by eggs and fries. "How can I help you?"

"You are a friend and. to me, that is important," she said after sitting across from him, with a similar plateful of food.

"Great cooking," he noted. "Thank you."

"Today we'll both go to the casino," she observed. "I have to work and you have a car to get."

"And a journey to continue," he added. "Amazing to meet you on my way to a park where you were a ranger."

"Coffee's ready," she said, getting up and walking to the counter. She returned to place a steaming mug in front of Ray and another across from him before she sat down again.

"Good service in this restaurant," he said, before picking up the mug. "In a way, I'm already at the park because I have met you."

"There's no such thing as coincidence," she replied. "I know the park and you. When you come back from this journey, your third lifetime will begin.

It will be different from the others only because you will have discovered you."

"Will I be disappointed?" he asked.

"No," she said. "I haven't been."

"Did you get as knowledgeable as you are by working at the park?" he inquired.

"Yes," she answered. "I went there lost and I was found, by me."

"Sounds to be a special place," he stated.

"It's over ninety five percent natural wilderness with much of that being old growth forest," she restated. "This is the home and work of the Creator so in this place you will find not only forms of life but spiritual life. That's the greatest gift Olympic National Park can give to any visitor."

"You are so much more than a casino employee," he said, staring at her. "I'm so pleased to have met you."

Standing up, she said, "I'll refill your mug and maybe we could go outside to finish coffee before returning to the casino."

"OK," he replied, standing.

Outside, they sat on chairs facing eastward toward the rising sun.

"A new day begins," he noted.

"We are each to the other a sign post along the way to show us we are exactly where we should be on our journeys to return back to the spiritual world," she outlined.

"The more I listen to you, the more amazed I become to see some of this world where we live," he observed.

"Being strong is not enough," she said. "We have to know we're strong and that's what the park will do for you."

They watched a coyote walk toward them. The visitor picked up some food then turned around and slowly moved out of sight.

"You feed coyotes?" he asked.

"Yes," she answered. "There are also coyotes in the park along with gray wolves, also known as timber wolves."

"Timber wolves aren't mentioned in the pamphlets," he noted.

"A lot of things are not listed in the pamphlets," she replied. "As I keep saying, the park is over ninety-five percent natural wilderness so that means it's over ninety-five percent unexplored and unknown. The spiritual world is also not mentioned in the brochures. The spiritual world is what I discovered and those of us who have really seen this presence are never the same again. Life is an unending opportunity but while we are on earth most of what we see is trouble. That's what we came here to experience because there's nothing close to that to learn from in the spirit world of the Creator. Wilderness is the Creator's garden. No human could ever plant a garden similar to the Olympic National Park."

"Wow and I'm going there," he whispered.

"We were intended to meet," she said. "Upon meeting, we made the right choices and are both on the correct trail of life. We know this by the sign posts and maybe now we should return to the casino."

They drove back in silence. After they left the car and entered the building, Ray asked, "How do I thank you for all you have been?"

"You don't," she replied, "and I'll never forget you, either."

They walked away and Ray returned to the rented room. In a short time, he was packed. Before leaving the casino, he purchased a takeout coffee along with muffins then walked to his car.

After placing each item in the vehicle, he started traveling again, entering a desert landscape patterned with Joshua trees. Passing cars were so few in number that the people in them waved to each other as they went by. Once, behind Ray's vehicle there seemed to occur an increasingly loud tearing sound just before his car was buzzed by a fighter jet flown by a pilot who, as a driver of a car, must have been attracted to the sight of a vehicle moving along the road.

Leaving Nevada and entering California, Ray drove through Death Valley. In a middle section, he parked on a lot, stepped out of his car and found the heat to be so intense, the air was thick and had a physical presence. Following this furnace experience, he drove onward to higher ground and more normal temperatures.

He kept traveling onward without stopping for any length of time until he came to Trees of Mystery in Klamath. Here there were redwood trees over 1,000 years old and more than 300 feet tall. Almost as amazing, were the giant Sitka spruce along with western hemlocks, Douglas firs and cedars.

He stayed for one night at a motel in Crescent City. Fog filled the darkness and through the mist came sounds of ship foghorns, in addition to calls from sea lions.

The next day, after breakfast and visiting a harbor where early morning fishermen were filleting a large catch of tuna, he started his journey again, stopping at a motel at Cannon Beach, Oregon. Walking through the town, he entered a butcher shop and bought a steak. At another shop, he got a piece of blackberry pie, in addition to some onions.

Back at the room, he cooked a great meal. Afterward he turned on the gas fireplace and sat beside it to enjoy some beer, while watching the beach.

Seeing the sun approaching the horizon, he went outside, walked to the water then turned southward to proceed along the beach. Waves pounded down into shallow water as Ray looked in the opposite direction and saw windows of shoreline buildings painted gold by rays from the setting sun. *The realm of the sea is a world and wilderness of its own,* Ray mused while he walked with golden light on each side of a seemingly endless coastline.

Gold is fading as the day is ending, he observed. *I should get back to the resort.* He slept soundly in the room and greeted the next morning by walking back to the town to get several muffins and coffee.

Traveling again, he did not have much time for treats before he came to the Columbia River. He visited a fish hatchery and watched large salmon swim along a fish ladder. Next, he visited the restored

Fort Clatsop where the Lewis and Clark expedition wintered from 1805-1806.

Leaving the fort, Raylon entered Washington State then drove into Olympic National Park. *There are three different regions in the park, including the coast, temperate rain forest and mountains,* recalled Ray. *I'll start by visiting the coast.*

He resumed driving and chose a campsite by the coast. After setting up his tent and camp, he purchased sandwiches along with beer and other items to complete his list of supplies. With packs well equipped and carrying a walking stick, he left his camp.

"This is what I came here to see," he shouted, as he walked toward the beach. *Definitely this is low tide,* he noted, upon seeing swells crashing a short distance out from shore and leaving a border of wet sand where he could walk. The route wound among numerous rocks and logs along with some whole trees. *There's a constant pounding of waves crashing down on sand,* observed Ray. *Against this background there are cries of gulls and terns. A salty scent is in the air mixed with a fragrance of fish.*

I'm finally here, he repeated a thought while walking quickly, following sections of smooth, wet sand bordered by rocks and occasional walls of logs and trees.

I've walked until I'm tired, he thought, *because it's such a wonderful change from so much driving. Time has come to rest and enjoy a snack.*

He sat on a log, rested his back against another then opened a package of sandwiches accompanied by juice. *I'm here, at my destination,* he thought again. *I'll save all containers and burn them when I have a fire. Right now, I'm going to have some beer and just enjoy being here.*

Awakened by water around his feet, Ray was shocked and wondered where he was until he remembered walking along the coast. *High tide has trapped me up against the driftwood,* he realized. *Maybe I could walk behind all this driftwood at the back of the beach. Night has also arrived. I'll move to dry sand beyond or among logs and uprooted trees then try to get more sleep before morning.*

Picking a new location, he felt comfortable and was rested by the sound of pounding waves until he was again sleeping soundly. In the morning, he welcomed a new day with its promise of escape because of low tide.

Having his packs in place and walking stick in his hand, he was about to start walking to the beach when he saw the bear. *The possibility of seeing a bear was mentioned only once in a brochure,* he recalled. *The bears in this park are supposed to be only black and this giant is definitely brown.* The bear left the sand and rushed toward gulls circling over a large fish struggling at the surface. Calling sharply, the birds flew higher while the intruder clamped jaws on the fish then started bringing it to shore.

The giant stopped, stood up on back legs and dropped the fish on sand before raking the air with one paw as if trying to determine what had been detected. Apparently making a decision, the hunter returned all paws to the sand and charged Ray.

Knowing running was useless, Ray could only wait, holding the only weapon he had and that was the walking stick. Worse than any nightmare, Ray watched as the bear bounded forward, stopping only when directly in front of Ray. Standing again on back legs, the giant roared and raked the air with one paw before slamming Ray with the other. Ray saw a blur of movement from the side. A light flashed, followed immediately by darkness.

Ray regained consciousness with a pounding headache. Light filtered through debris piled overhead. *The bear has partially buried me,* noted Ray. *The giant is saving me for later. He was starting with the fish and I suppose I interrupted his meal. That's not a good time to get in the way of a bear, particularly a grizzly. If low tide is here, I'll resume traveling.*

He pushed aside the covering of sand and wood, looked out at the water and saw a chance to leave with the return of a border of wet sand stretching out to waves. They rolled forward, crested then crashed down, breaking into foaming turbulence. Delayed only by a headache in addition to soreness along the side of his face and one shoulder, he hurried back along the beach.

After reaching his tent, he set up the propane-fueled stove and boiled vegetable soup. Pouring some into a bowl, he added crushed crackers then thought, *this is the best meal when I'm recovering from something. I also have biscuits I'll top with honey before resting until my headache vanishes. Soreness should soon leave my face and shoulder. When the critter hit me, claws left marks on my face in addition to cutting abrasions across my shoulder. I've put ointment on them and applied bandages. Fish was the main course for the beachcomber. I was saved maybe for dessert or a snack.*

Having finished the meal and resting, Ray decided to continue relaxing while adding a few extra supplies. He decided to drive and check places to obtain equipment and food. As a last stop, he parked in front of an out of the way mercantile just beyond the park. He entered the building and immediately knew he had, in one place, an answer to all his possible requirements.

"Holler if you need help," said a woman who was working at a desk behind a central counter. She was slim, seeming to be all muscle. Closely cropped black hair bordered her attractive face, showing strength. Her eyes were black yet slightly brown. She seemed to present a direct approach to life and would tolerate no schemes. Of the visitor who had just entered her store, she first noticed his greenish-blue eyes. His hair had been black and was now graying. His stature was either strong or getting there.

"Thank you," replied Ray. "You have here all the supplies I or anyone could possibly need to camp or just journey into Olympic National Park. The food, particularly, stands out as being as unique as it is fresh."

"The food in this store is either ranch or farm raised," she explained. "Nothing is wild."

"Fish and other meats look particularly good, both fresh and frozen," he noted.

"If something isn't good, I know where it came from," she stated.

"What do you think is the best, tastiest fish?" asked Ray.

"Most people would say salmon because they haven't tried Arctic char," she replied. "Of course the trout, char, salmon and even white fish are all part of the same salmon family. My favorite fish is Arctic char. Traditionally, our people, the Quinault, have included wild goat and sheep for food. I sell ranched goat and sheep meat, keeping our traditions."

"What is your name?" he asked.

"Lily," she answered, "and your name?"

"Ray, actually Raylon James," he replied. "Looks as if you sell good firewood here and propane."

"Yes," she said. "This to me is more than a business. I see it as an effort to give people the best of what they need at the lowest possible price. I keep our traditions too. This place has Quinault life kept for today. Our ways are now the way they have been since records can be kept. For as long as has been remembered, we have been part of this region with its great mountains, forests and sea."

"I had the impression this place was more than a store," he said.

"When you walked in here," she said, "I had the impression you were here by design beyond our planning. We are intended to meet as links in wonderful outcomes for both of us."

"When something is right, I should not hesitate but get started," he said, before picking out some frozen Arctic char along with cans of different types of baked beans. Lastly, he added ice.

"Good choices," she said, after he paid by credit card and she had butcher-wrapped the meat along with placing all items in a paper bag.

"This will be a great day for grilling some Arctic char," he said while walking toward the door.

"Thanks for your visit and business," she added, before he stepped outside. Having placed the package in the trunk of his car, he opened the driver's door, got inside, sat down and started the motor. *My journey in this park,* he thought, *has just started.*

Back at his tent, he unloaded his parcel then walked to the beach. *It's low tide so I must explore,* he decided.

Using a fast stride, he followed firm, damp sand surrounding numerous, large rocks. Farther back, along the shore, there were piles of drift logs mixed occasionally with whole trees.

When I first arrived along this beach, he recalled, *I found it to be cold, harsh and threatening. Now I feel I've just arrived and see for the first time the greater beauty of this shore with constantly changing patterns of big sky, distant mountains, drift logs, looming rocks and miles of sand. These parts are joined not into competing sections but one life, breathing in and out, always moving in arrival or departure, as each aspect flows in harmony and belongs with all the others.*

Upon my arrival, the bear showed me I didn't belong because I had not taken time to understand or appreciate what was here and I intruded without respect, he thought. *Now, I not only have respect but I'm in awe of this place where each section is powerful and, in its own way, works together in a special expression of connected life. This is a living coast and it's one of a kind. I now belong and am no longer an intruder.*

In front of Ray, there was a person sitting on a chair beside an extra chair with a table in front of it. On it a plate had been placed topped by some food. The man was fishing, holding a fishing pole as line extended out into surf.

"Another beautiful day," said Ray, after approaching the person. His hair was white, face somewhat tanned but most noticeable were his bright, greenish-blue eyes.

"Every day has this quality if we can see it," replied the man. "Please sit down and try some fish I've prepared for you."

"You caught and cooked as I approached?" asked Ray.

"You did all this," said the man. "Today you accepted what you first saw as cold, harsh and rough; so now this land and water can accept you and let you in. You will never be the same again. You are one of us. Each part is not separate but only a different aspect where there is the connection of the Creator. Today you did not turn your back but you accepted and all life celebrates."

"You sound like a pastor," observed Ray.

"Yes," replied the man. "Try some fish."

Ray tried the food then finished the sample and said, "That is the best fish I've ever tasted."

"Enjoy the food you buy from Lily," said the man. "She knows who you are. Today you accepted and thereby are no longer separate but have come home. Just believe in the Creator, accept, and trouble will not harm you; but there will always be trouble."

"I just came to this park to get stronger," explained Ray. "Now, I find I'm not only strong but am actually part of this place and its life."

"The Christian churches bring people to the Creator," said the man. "There are other churches and ways to accept the Creator. Just like walking a beach, seeing more than sand and, today, you accepted and returned home to the Creator."

Feeling a new understanding of the land, water, and air, Ray looked around, seeing for the first time and knew he would never feel alone again. All the surroundings seemed to jump closer emblazoned with light that included him.

When Ray turned back to thank the man, he was gone and everything he had with him had also vanished. *Days will be good in the future,* thought Raylon, *but no day will be this good again. I've not just visited this place I've joined it.*

As a person in a dream, he walked back to his tent. He started a fire in the place provided. On a skewer, he grilled some Arctic char, bringing the meat to a golden-brown color.

He sat on his folding chair, enjoyed the food then looked out toward the Pacific. Lastly he poured beer into a draft glass and started sipping the refreshing drink. The sun was dipping into a layer of fog along the horizon, tinting both sky and water with a golden sheen. As the sun moved lower, gold turned to red before the orb vanished amid darkening colors of night. When night was almost present, a great horned owl called from the shadows.

Ray refilled the glass. Moonlight was brightening the landscape when, in this light, he carried his full glass to the edge of dry sand. Resting at this location, he watched swells move toward shore, stand up, crest then fall with a thunderous crash upon the beach. Wave after wave, from the silver sea, thundered ashore. With this company, Ray went to sleep.

He awoke in first light of dawn when he saw a coyote approaching. The traveler picked up a small fish at the water's edge and this treat was being crunched when the coyote noticed Ray.

Yellow eyes focused on Ray briefly before an apparently old trail was resumed and the beachcomber continued walking along the shore. *The coyote is right,* thought Ray, standing. *Time has come for some breakfast.*

After starting a fire in the pit, he fried some eggs, toasted two slices of bread and made a toasted, fried egg sandwich. Afterward, he washed dishes while the coffee pot perked. Sitting on his favorite folding chair, he sipped coffee in preparation for the new day.

Amid pastel hues of dawn, he drove to a bait and tackle shop. He entered a small room, smelling of fish, where the proprietor appeared to have just crawled out of the ocean himself and was thereby an authority on all things about the sea. Green eyes looked out from an overgrown thicket comprised of hair, eyebrows and beard. To this apparently knowledgeable fellow, Ray explained, "I asked park rangers and they recommended catching surfperch as a best type of fishing. Bait could be razor clam necks or plastic sand worms. I'd like to get a package of both along with recommended perch hooks, some two-once sand sinkers, a pair of hip waders, a belt to go around the outside of them and, lastly, a state fishing license. The advice I received was to place the sinker at the end of the line with a hook up about two to three feet. Hip waders are required because the water is cold. A belt around the outside keeps the waders from filling completely, knocking me off balance and tumbling me into waves. The line is cast out into foaming water behind breaking waves. Surfperch are large enough for good filleting and fine eating. Because there are many surfperch, catch limits are high, twelve a day, unlike other fish in the park. All wild fish are catch and release."

"You've been well advised," stated the man with the small amount of face showing amid the foliage. "I can't improve on your advice but I can get your stuff ready for you so fast you'll think I knew you were coming and raised the prices; but no, I didn't raise the prices for you, I doubled them for everyone."

"You're a real fisherman," replied Ray. "We have to cut facts in half to get around to what is really being said. It's a type of fishing language."

"Always good to meet a member of the clan," added the guy before he returned to his mouth a cigar butt he apparently kept saving a long time by not lighting it.

"Would large waders work?" asked the guy.

"Yes," answered Ray.

"Your order is ready and I've doubled the price too," stated the guy.

"Sounds fair," noted Ray, as he paid his bill then said, "Almost forgot the Washington State recreational fishing license for fishing in the Pacific Ocean from shore."

"We'll take care o' that right now," proclaimed the proprietor. He tried, although failed to light the stub of cigar before starting the process for the license. Upon completion, he said, "Always good to have a license; and may the sea and fish bring you wonderful days."

"You help people to enjoy them," added Ray, before he left the shop. He drove to a beach where one other person was fishing about half a mile away.

Ray put on the waders then assembled his fishing pole. He tied a two-once sand sinker to the end of the line with a hook up about two and a half feet. For bait he started with a chunk of razor clam necks. He buried the hook, leaving only the barbed end protruding.

I feel at home now, he thought. *This is the same hook and sinker setup I use in Florida coastal fishing with a two-once sand sinker at the end of the line and a hook up about two and a half to three feet. Most other Florida coastal fishermen put the hook at the end of the line and sinker up from it. Such a rig places the bait on the bottom. I keep the bait up off the bottom to avoid bottom feeders, such as stingrays and catfish.*

With a plastic bag for fish tied to his belt, he waded out to meet onrushing remnants of waves.

Above the sea, gulls called to a panorama of water and sky.

Walking to where the larger swells were breaking, he tossed his line out to drop into churning water left by crashing crests. Immediately there was a bite on the bait and a struggle started. Ray wound in line while backing away from remnants of waves. He reeled in a large surfperch that although somewhat rounder in shape was similar to perch anywhere. A blend of silver, yellow and green colors flashed in sunlight.

After unhooking this first catch, he dropped the fish into a bag at his side then waded out again to meet the sea. *The day is perfect for fishing,* he noted before again tossing the baited line out beyond breaking crests. *All wild birds, animals and fish enjoy the same weather people prefer,* noted Ray. *They also run for cover during storms. Even fish act differently in rough weather. When I was fishing in Florida during strong winds, mackerel swam close to shore.*

The pole bent and throbbed after another perch struck the bait. Always seeming to be larger in battle than the fish's actual size, the next catch entered shallow water to quickly join the first fish in the bag.

One more if the sea and fish are willing, thought Ray, while walking again to toss the line into foaming water behind breaking rollers. The third strike led to another battle larger than the fish and gave Ray a sufficient supply for at least two of the finest possible fish dinners.

Stopping to look at his surroundings, he observed, *fishing is so much more than getting fillets for food. The frying of fillets is just part of enjoying the memory of, for a short time, becoming part of the environment including the sea where swells rush onward, hit shallow water then crest and crash into a churning border where fish dart for food. Sound is important. Waves usually don't come in broken patterns but in uniformity resulting in continuous sound and its naturalness is more soothing and restful than any other music. To this background, gulls call, adding their voices to ancient patterns. There is also a visual component to the spell cast by the sea where sunlight dances on breaking crests along with painting passing clouds and adding warmth to dispel coolness of the water. The panorama of water, sky, and land, although constantly changing, remain within ancient patterns, creating a world of constant interest and beauty. There is so much more to fishing than getting fillets. Just picking up fillets would be easier to do today in a grocery store. In earlier times, people caught fish because this food was needed for survival. Today, because generally there are more fishermen than fish can supply, laws are needed to save wild fish. Wild fish in Olympic National Park, aside from surfperch that remain in good supply, are for catch and release only. Where fish can't supply the demand for them, such particular food must come from fish farms. Fishermen have to go to a grocery store for food and only enter the wilderness to get fish, such as surfperch that are in sufficient supply to meet the demand. The world of fishing is so much larger than just a search for meat.*

Back at camp, he filleted the fish, placed extra parts in a dumpster provided for such items then he shook the fillets in a bag containing corn meal. He fried these special pieces in vegetable oil until they were golden brown on both sides.

Ray placed these items on a plate, splashed them with some malt vinegar followed by sprinklings of salt and pepper. When all preparations had been completed, he sat down to enjoy a banquet to match and go beyond what was available in any restaurant. Savoring the food, he thought, *the meat is white and has a trace of flavor like perch anywhere along with bass, walleye, or Florida's mackerel.*

Following the meal, he walked to the coast and watched the setting sun paint sky and ocean with a last flare of reddish hues before encroaching shadows became the night. In a short time, this realm was again brightened by returning colors—this time cast from the moon appearing to break away from the horizon and gradually climb the sky and eventually cover the physical world with a silver sheen. Ray returned to his tent and enjoyed a deep sleep, made possible not just by fatigue but also by his mind being content with his present journey.

Morning light came early, finding Ray ready to greet or start a new adventure. After perking coffee, he sat to enjoy a cup of the stimulating drink. From it, steam drifted and, as he watched the coast receive light, he thought, *there is the promise of each new day. Like all the others, each one comes to offer its special opportunity and will never come back again. After each of these single segments of opportunity has been completed, a life ends. Upon looking back upon a life, some individuals say they would do it all over again, changing nothing. I never would make such a statement. I would not want to repeat any of my mistakes or failures, nor many of the hardships.*

After breakfast, at low tide, Ray started a long walk along the shore. His journey continued until the tide started to return. *I don't know what the rules are here,* he thought, *but time has come for me to have some sort of a shower.* Quickly removing his clothes, standing in shallow water, he used sand along with a small amount of environmentally approved soap and scrubbed from head to toe. Cleaning was completed with a rinse. He returned to the shore where he put on again all his clothes before he rushed back to the area where he was camped, successfully avoiding the rising tide.

He sat on a border of dry sand and watched the tide come to shore. He was not the only watcher. Gulls were resting to his right and left. They, too, were part of the changing sea.

When I first came here, I was a stranger, he recalled. *The bear found me to be an intruder, not much more than food. A different situation is here now. I have come home and I know home is not just here but everywhere there is a natural wilderness. It is not just physical but spiritual. In returning, we are always accepted.*

Ray gathered his fishing equipment and caught a spirit of excitement in returning to the place where previously he had caught surfperch. He put on the waders, including the belt then prepared the fishing pole with its hook and sinker. This time, for bait, he used plastic sand worms.

With equipment ready, he waded into breaking waves then cast the baited line out to fall into churning water behind a long crashing swell. He joined the song of the sea, played constantly and, in its continuity, added an atmosphere of restfulness Ray sought as much or much more than food. Colors too were gathering, brightening as the sun started its descent to the horizon.

A strike on the line jolted Ray's attention away from colors on water and sky and back to what was under the surface. *Sand worms work as well as razor clam necks,* he noted while reeling in a large, battling surfperch. It was larger than the previous catches. This fish had just been dropped into the bag when there followed another fish of similar size. *Today,* observed Ray, while he walked back to his car, *the sea abounds with fish.*

He filleted this new catch and started preparations for one of the best of meals. While the fillets sizzled in vegetable oil in a pan placed on a grill above a steadily burning fire, Ray added a slight amount of the same oil to a second pan. He placed it at the edge of the heat rather than directly in it where the fish cooked. Next he selected one of the tomatoes he had purchased at Lily's store. He picked one that was orange in color rather than red and had a haze of remnant green, the first start of ripeness. He cut off thick slices then placed each one in the pan. They were well seared or partly cooked before being placed on a separate dish to accompany a plateful of golden fried fillets. After the addition of salt and pepper, the finest of meals followed. *Fried tomatoes to accompany golden fillets,* thought Ray, *provid a wonderful treat to be enjoyed within sound of crashing waves. I could always stay at the coast. Maybe though, I should visit another part of home and get a campsite in the temperate rain forest. I'll do that today, online, and move tomorrow. For a meal tonight, I should grill Arctic char. I'll boil and fry some potatoes. I'll also pick some of the abundant black berries.*

Night brought a banquet to celebrate a successful homecoming to the coast and the next day to continue with the same home yet in a different region, the rain forest. On my *way to the new campsite tomorrow,* he decided, *I'll visit Lily's store and fill any remaining space in the car with firewood. I'll even put on the roof racks and pile as much wood as possible. Lots of firewood will help to keep my next camping place dry.*

Following the meal, he packed for the next day before he walked to the coast and sat on the border of dry sand. *As we measure time,* he observed, *I haven't been at this coast long enough to enter it; but, in fact, I have traveled much further than time would count for I've become part of this place. I'm going to miss the companionship of booming surf as great swells come toward shore, crest then crash, sending out flows of water while stirring up food for surfperch. There's also the company of changing colors through deep hues as the sun rises to paleness of midday before sky, water and land reveal again the always-present tints before the completion of the cycle. Mainly though, I'll miss the sound of the ocean along with its great size, power and grandeur. This park is a place of extremes from the vast openness of the sea to the wet abundance of rain forest and also lofty mountains.*

Sunlight next morning warmed Lily and Ray while they assessed the load of firewood tied to the top of Ray's car.

"You're the type of customer who makes my work so interesting," exclaimed Lily, before she turned to go back to the store.

"Your business is essential for the present frontier," replied Ray, "We can no longer take food and supplies from the forest. There are too many people needing supplies and too little wilderness to supply them. Your store provides everything I and others can no longer harvest ourselves."

"You have just explained why I'm so dedicated to my work," exclaimed Lily. "I'm saving the wilderness and just haven't, until now, put words to the essential work my business and other stores are doing. Thank you."

"I appreciate the fact your supplies are of good quality, reliable and guaranteed," said Ray. "Having obtained a carload of good products, I can now go to the temperate rain forest."

"See you soon," added Lily, before she walked back to her store.

Ray got into his car. Rather than rushing onward, he stopped to consider his actions. Recalling his progress so far, he thought, *I'm starting the next part of my journey to get stronger, although I've recently discovered the strength was already in me. All I had to do was become aware of it and unlock it.*

The sun kept shining while he drove to his new campsite in the rain forest. Light clouds drifted in a blue sky as he parked his car. A symphony of singing hermit thrush came from walls of greenery surrounding a small clearing where the campsite was established.

Ray first set up his tent, as he always did, having it face the fire pit but back far enough to allow space for his chair placed between the fire pit and tent. Next he put up the tarpaulin to have it cover much of the tent then stretch over the front reaching to the middle of where the fire would be sending up flames. Reviewing his finished camp, he noted, *the tarp will keep the front area of the tent dry, while protecting the fire so it will not get extinguished even during some of the approximately twelve feet of yearly precipitation that, in spite of the present sunshine is on the way.*

On a skewer, he prepared a piece of Arctic char while a sharpened sapling held a chunk of sheep or mutton all purchased from Lily's store. After cooking preparations had been completed, he sat on his chair, placed where it would always be in front of the tent and under the tarp.

I'm home again, he thought, before sipping beer. *I'm in a different part of home but all regions are connected. I'll miss the coast yet can continue to have it with me in memory while a new section of the park opens. I have the camp set for rain, including a good supply of firewood, kept dry under tarps. I have also purchased a special raincoat and hat. There's comfort in knowing I have a good supply of food along with some beer to celebrate the evenings. The temperate rain forest can send its customary precipitation because I'm ready.*

As evening was approaching, Ray lit some wood shavings in the firepit. The flame climbed among kindling then swarmed over larger pieces. A fire was soon burning steadily bringing heat to skewered Arctic char. It sizzled while fat dripped from a chunk of mutton held above the flames by a stick.

Such meals have been prepared for countless years, reflected Ray, while he watched the food approach its most tender and delicious stage. *I can't hunt to get this food because there now are too many hunters and not enough natural or wild places to supply them; however, the foods are kept available through farming and ranching. Wild birds and animals can also continue to live and enjoy their lives without being shot by hunters. I notice two deer are watching my food preparations. They and other parts of the wild carry on with their lives while people can get food abundantly from stores. Not all people accept time has forced a change in our ways of getting food. Places, such as the Olympic National Park are a refuge not just for people but all parts of life, including animals, birds and trees.*

In company with the steadily burning fire and surrounding forest, Ray savored the meal in a way such food had been prepared and enjoyed since records had been kept on this land. After the meal, he cleaned his few utensils, sat on the folding chair, sipped some beer and continued appreciating this new region of home.

As expected, the rain came. A first few drops tapped against tent and tarp just before a deluge struck. A sheet of spray filled the world outside the area protected by the tarpaulin. Within this zone, flames continued to stand up on wood, bringing brightness and dryness to the camp.

We have to live with the environment and not against it, reflected Ray, while he enjoyed the scene of fire and water. Gradually the downpour dwindled to a pleasant tapping of drops against the tarp and tent. Such music helped bring to Ray comfort of a deep sleep.

In the morning, he prepared porridge accompanied by a piece of toast topped by strawberry jam and another with honey. Three cups of coffee were worked in while he prepared his usual traveling equipment, including a backpack filled with supplies and snacks. To these items, he added a raincoat and hat.

Using the car to change from one location to another, Ray prepared to walk along trails. He carried a walking stick and started to enjoy the rain, considering it to be a companion. Water dripped from the surrounding forest. Through mist and rain, birds sang and moved as another feature of forest where innumerable, different, separate parts lived together as one life, breathing in and out.

After following established paths, Ray noticed side trails that maybe long ago had been routes followed by people through thousands of years of life. In addition, there were game trails used by residents, such as deer, elk, and black bear.

One morning, Ray carried a folding chair along with a cup and thermos filled with coffee. He followed a game as well as possibly early human trail. It led him away from the areas most often traveled or seen by people during modern times. While stepping through a green panorama of life, he thought, *back through the records of people in this region, one of the most remembered of all the newcomers, there was the record of Captain James Cook who visited Nootka Sound on Vancouver Island in March 29, 1778. He was known as a captain to whom things happened. He started a trade, whereby English and Americans wanted furs, particularly of the sea otter. They were traded in China where sea otter furs were highly prized. The coastal people of Canada traded furs in return for many items although the most cherished of them all was copper.*

Ray unfolded his chair and sat. From the pack, he removed a thermos along with mug he filled with coffee. *If I stop moving,* he thought, *I become more aware of other parts of the rain forest as they continue to be active. When a person sits in a human-made building, the person sees only surroundings that are not alive. Sitting here in this forest and looking around, I observe countless living parts and they are all moving, growing in complexity and harmony more miraculous by far than any human-made building. Yet people cut down these forests to build lesser things too often considered more valuable and much more expensive.*

So far, I've seen a stellar jay and Canada jay, for a short time *known as gray jay, pileated woodpecker, magpie, crow and raven. The forest is*

119

*filled with music from birds I'm not sure of
identifying although I know I've detected thrushes,
such as the hermit and robin in addition to warblers.
Of the birds, a frequent singer is the red-eyed vireo.*

Ray refilled his cup then sipped some of the strong brew not garnished by cream or sugar. While trying to not think about all he was seeing but just enjoy it, a light flashed through the scene and he saw that everything was connected in this spiritual light or presence of the Creator. Remarkably, Ray suddenly became aware again that he and all people who had not turned away were included. All parts were together and the light was present, although more noticeable during some occasions than others.

When the light went back to the way the forest usually looked, Ray knew he had been allowed a special moment, a vision. He closed his eyes and enjoyed the occasion. When he opened his eyes again, he had a view of the forest a traveler using one of the main trails would not observe. He saw an unusually square shape among branches of a massive Sitka spruce.

Ray walked to the tree and started climbing. Proceeding upward, he thought, *branches are close together and evenly spaced so I can easily step from one to another almost as a stairway.* He came to the unusual shape and realized it was a very old, moss-covered cabin.

He went inside the structure, discovering he was back in time many years. *This place,* he thought, *was made a long time ago and by an expert woodworker. I should not intrude but I'll draw a map to clearly indicate how to get here. I'll mention this discovery to Lily. She will look after the information herself or know someone who keeps records about the traditions of the Quinault.*

Walking back to his tent camp, Ray sat on his chair facing the fire pit and recalled, *there are six hundred miles of trails in this park. It is an area mainly of trails. Today I have journeyed beyond where anyone usually travels on these trails. I've been many years back through time to a cabin built during the early years of the region of this park and by one of the first people to live here. I've also been into the spirit world where life will continue after the*

*physical part of the earth has gone. My next journey
will be to the mountains.*

Ray visited Lily's store. Smiling, Lily said, "Welcome to one who belongs here."

"Thank you," he replied. "That's a wonderful greeting."

"One that I don't use often," she said.

"I feel at home here, as I enjoy the forest," he observed. "I can be inside your store and continue to have the feeling I haven't left the forest."

"That's the greatest compliment you could give," she exclaimed, as her face brightened.

"In addition to needing more supplies, I brought you a message from someone who likely lived in a Quinault village, when people first inhabited this area. You will either look after the message yourself or send it off to another person. I found an old cabin built in a Sitka spruce and now the structure is moss covered." Giving her the sketch of the cabin along with directions, indicating how to reach the site, Ray said, "I made this detailed outline of the cabin and its location. The person who built the structure was likely also trained as an expert canoe builder."

"This is most likely a very important part of our past," she replied. "I'll send it out to one of our tradition keepers. We cherish people who restore our past. Thank you for giving me this information."

"Our story is far from complete," said Ray. "For the next part of my exploration of the park, I'm going to the mountains."

"The coast, temperate rain forest and mountains, might seem different to those who don't realize the environment has only one builder," observed Lily. "The three sections of the park all have immense grandeur and power together with the smallest and most delicate of parts of life. There is only one land, water and sky although they have different characteristics in various areas."

"There's so much more than I'll ever understand but I, mostly the same as you, have all I need to know and that is the importance of staying with the Creator and not turning away," said Ray. "To help follow the right journey, there are messengers as Christ."

"You know what is essential," replied Lily. "The rest is the small stuff of life, the obstacles that hone each person's spirit."

"You have a lot more here than supplies," stated Ray.

"Not everyone notices," she replied. "I particularly enjoy those who notice."

"So do I," he said. "Now for some of the less important stuff, I have items to purchase; but you are the best at everything you provide."

"Wow," she exclaimed. "Thanks."

With new supplies, including a wood-burning stove for the tent along with a pipe to extend through the roof, Ray left the store. He started a new exploration taking him to the mountains with the snow-topped peaks, forested slopes and green valleys, often broken by rivers or lakes.

He prepared a new camp on a remote site and from there he set out on extended walks that became longer with each journey. Gathering suitable experience to feel he was at home again, he enjoyed his camp when he was there.

While preparing goat meat on sapling poles for roasting over the fire pit, he said to himself, *I have shopped at the store to get all my camp requirements. There was a time when hunters were few and wild game seemed to be unlimited. Today hunters are numerous while creatures and land have dwindled until the wilderness is not able to provide required supplies. People can no longer harvest what they do not sow. If they don't plant it, they can't pick it. If they don't farm or ranch it, they can't kill it. Fish are different because of restocking from hatcheries. Today laws are required to make sure each person fishes respectfully, not taking more than what can be sustained. The contemporary wilderness is for life not just to supply food or logs. I'm dining on goat as hunters did in the past but I acquired this food from the store and the meat came from a ranch. I have made preparations and tomorrow I'm going to walk farther than ever before to see what new territory is available for me to discover. I've become accustomed to going beyond the established routes. Curiosity leads every exploration. I always want to see what is over the next hill then beyond that to the next and each time I reach a destination, I see only more intriguing realms extending into blue mist. Such curiosity has not yet led to the full discovery of the earth or people on it but is sending some adventurers to consider traveling to the Moon, Mars and farther.*

The next morning arrived with an extra edge to the wind, part of the coldest day to arrive with the first signs of winter that comes early to the high country. For breakfast, Ray made porridge garnished with raisins and topped by brown sugar. Having all the ingredients ready for mixing, he was surprised to see jays helping themselves to the raisins.

All brochures, he recalled, *instruct people not to feed wildlife. Park rules don't mention wild residents helping themselves to food preparations. These jays are Canada jays. Woodsmen have for a long time called them camp robbers.*

After placing raisins on his hand, Ray held out this treat to the jays. They immediately swooped in, landed on his hand and picked up the offered food. Chickadees joined the feast.

What a wonderful beginning to a new day and my intention to travel outside any established route, concluded Ray. Having all preparations completed, including a pack on his back and a walking stick, he started traveling along only slightly visible paths. They became more obscure with the approach of night.

Forced to stop, he looked into the cooling vastness of sky where colors following sunset were fading as grayness darkened. *I'm beyond any trail,* he noted. *I would now be outside park boundaries.*

He stretched out the tarpaulin to form the roof of a lean-to sheltering an air mattress covered by an eider down sleeping bag. In front of this shelter, he started a fire then sharpened sticks to roast the evening meal. *Tonight,* he decided, *I'm going to grill salmon and heat biscuits to be garnished with honey or jam. The fish I purchase from Lily's store are Arctic char. I think Arctic char is the finest of all foods.*

After the biscuits were heated then topped by honey or jam, the fish was grilled until it turned to a dark, brownish-gold color. *Delicious food,* reflected

Ray after he finished savoring both the fish and biscuits. *All items for food preparation are burnable, including containers for the beer I'm going to enjoy, now.*

Ray sat in front of the lean-to. Warmed by the fire, he looked beyond its brightness to slight shadows of mountains becoming more visible as the moon appeared to climb the sky. A slight rustling of an errant breeze broke the silence generally only interrupted by snapping wood in the fire. A few sparks swirled upward before quickly vanishing. The howling of wolves rang clearly in the vastness, seeming to come from wild messengers close to camp. Howls were sent out and answered. Some came from Ray as he encouraged the cries of wilderness.

Silence returned broken again only by the snapping fire. When the flames started to diminish above coals, Ray slept soundly.

Next morning, in the first light of dawn, he coaxed a flame from coals to perk coffee. He also heated some biscuits then topped them with honey and greeted the rising sun while he sipped coffee. The first, second and third cup of awakener brought his attention to the transformation the warming sun's rays gave to the mountains. Mist dissipated while colors brightened, bringing to life a world Ray was eager to explore.

While walking, he thought, *I feel as if I have new strength but actually, as the rising sun brings life to the mountains, this Olympic National Park has awakened strength I already had but, in the past, I did not know of its presence. The awareness is new and not the strength. I've had it all the time but now it fuels my outlook on life. The ruggedness of these mountains call to the person I have untapped in this park, having strength not from outside but in my spirit. Following such an awakening, I'm now called beyond established trails to new terrain, not usually visited by tourists. I don't even mind the increasing wind although the first snow and hail in it is hitting my face. Maybe I'll respond to the moment and walk among the wildest outcroppings of rock not only to respond to the call I feel toward them but, also there, I could find shelter until the driving sleet stops.*

Ray walked to a break in a craggy wall. This break, at closer range, became an opening and he walked inside. Light followed him from the outside as he continued onward, finding himself in an expansive cavern.

On a blackened area he assembled pieces of wood and relit them. He added larger chunks to the growing flames until he basked in warmth and light from the fire. He watched, as if caught in a spell from long lost days, as firelight danced across what must be treasures of the Quinault. On pounded panels of copper, some shaped as shields, there were crests in addition to other designs and symbols of the Quinault. What seemed to be most sensational were sheets of copper containing, outlined in symbols, the narrative history and traditions of the Quinault people. *Told in copper, there is the story of this region, the early days of Olympic National Park and what must be a prized record of the Quinault story,* observed Ray. *At the bottom of each piece of copper there is etched in symbol and English language the name of the worker, Gray Raven. This is treasure of the first people to live here and Olympic National*

Park. All of these works are accomplishments of Gray Raven. He must have died before he could bring his gifts to the people. Had he lived to see the presentation of his gifts he would have been present at a great potlatch or gift giving likely never seen before. He would have achieved high status for himself and his family. Such achievements would have brought him into a new lifetime. I'll have to report to Lily my discovery of this cave. This will add to the presence of the cabin in the Sitka spruce. She will know who to call to bring Gray Raven's great gifts to the people. Gray Raven died before he could complete such a wonderful part of his life. Maybe this is his third lifetime. I'm about to start my third lifetime, a period when I'm aware of my own strength and ability. Gray Raven didn't live to see this part of his life. I'm not superstitious but I also hope the same outcome doesn't happen to me. I have to get back to finish a third life time for myself and also for Gray Raven.

Preparing for the return journey, Ray warned himself, *I'm out of food. I'll have to sleep in this cave for the night and start my return journey in the morning.*

Next day's sunlight brought light to the mountains but any warmth was swept away by a breeze. Leaving the cave, Ray thought, *I'll have to travel as quickly as possible because I'm not only out of food but also water. I either didn't pack well or just traveled farther than expected. I have two lives to finish so I have to hurry. I keep trying to improve myself all the time, although some characteristics are more difficult to change than others. So far, I haven't been able to stop worrying. People are lucky who can take each circumstance as it comes then do what can be done without thinking about deep holes a person could fall into if correct procedures are not followed. Gray Raven did not live to see the great success of his third lifetime. I wonder if I not only discovered his success but will also realize the trails of our lives are the same. I wonder if I also will not live to see the success of my third lifetime.*

Trying unsuccessfully not to worry, Ray started walking back the way he had traveled. He stopped when he looked down into a meadow and saw five timber wolves bring down an elk.

I would like a grilled elk steak, he decided before he tried to get down to the ancient scene below. *I know all parts of life including people are unique and bonded together only by the spirit of the Creator. Variations might occur with individuals but wolves take sickness out of a herd of animals such as deer, elk, or buffalo. I know wolves were reintroduced to Yellowstone National Park and they took the sickness out of the herd of buffalo, thereby saving the herd at a time when killing the sick animals was being considered. The elk taken down now would not be in good condition. A steak would do me no harm and would supply some energy for my journey. There is a stream pouring down the side of the mountain and crossing this meadow. I could use food and water.*

As Ray approached the dead elk, the wolves backed away a short distance before stopping and turning to watch this intruder. At the elk's side, Ray looked at the wolves. They were motionless, as craggy parts of the mountains. *They belong here,* Ray warned himself. *I have also come to know the park as my home. This standoff will be a test to see if my new strength, awakened by these mountains, is a fact or just my imagination.*

Only gray, white and black fur moved, stirred by a fitful breeze. Yellow eyes watched Ray. Holding his hatchet in one hand and knife in the other, he cut away one steak. He speared it on his walking stick, returned the knife to its sheath and slowly backed away from the watching yellow eyes.

Having reached what should be a suitable distance, Ray started walking to the higher route. He kept looking back. The five wolves moved forward to get food.

After reaching the top of the slope, Ray drank from the stream. Feeling refreshed and having food to cook, he traveled again until he came to an area having sufficient wood for a fire. First he gathered fine twigs he placed on a base for the fire. Adding increasingly large pieces, he soon was ready to strike a match to start the blaze. A flame swarmed among dry pieces while Ray skewered meat on a stick he held in heat just above the flames. The food sizzled while dripping some fat into the fire.

Looking back, he thought, *while I cook a fine steak, the wolves would be enjoying their food. Ravens are calling and circling, waiting for their turn to visit the site.*

After a meal of roasted steak accompanied by water from the stream, Ray started walking as rapidly as possible. He raced approaching shadows. With vanishing sunlight came a cooler edge to the breeze. Colors in the sky faded, leaving only remnants of light patches, helping Ray get back to his camp. *It is too late to visit Lily at her store this evening,* he decided. *I'll stay here tonight and meet her in the morning.*

With tall flames of a fire burning in front of the tent, Raylon James looked beyond the flames to what he saw as his journey. *In my first lifetime,* he recalled, *I enjoyed my life but, when a test came, I wasn't prepared to meet it. My second lifetime is at Olympic National Park where I've discovered the strength I need to face life is actually in me and not something outside to be gathered inward. I'm now in my third lifetime, realizing trouble will always come but I have the strength, with spiritual guidance, to face each challenge.*

In this wilderness, of Olympic National Park, he repeated his thought; *I have found the strength I have sought. I have discovered it is not outside of me but inside. Trouble will keep coming. I now know I have the strength to face it. The elk back in the meadow had a complete journey in these mountains with the streams and meadows. Time came for this part to pass to others, mainly the five wolves. I would not have died without the food but the nourishment helped me get back to this camp. The wolves needed nourishment to survive. Trouble keeps coming but they face it and, in the overall workings of life, take illness out of the other animals. Sick animals become food. The scent of illness is transmitted to the wolves and these animals are also easier to catch. The wolves watched me and did not see me as particularly dangerous or weak. I faced trouble and got food but no more than was needed. The wilderness is a system in balance with all parts living and growing together. One life ends. Others begin or continue. The story is told. Gray Raven did not see his work reach his people. Now this will happen. One life ends. Others continue. I have found the strength I came here seeking. Now I can return. First however, I'll visit Lily and bring Gray Raven's work back to his people. Life is greater than we can see. Trouble will come. All we can do is our best, facing each obstacle, being the best we can be along the journey.*

Ray slept well and was up early. He prepared a small breakfast, consisting of the last biscuits completed by coffee. He was at the store in time to greet Lily when she arrived.

"That's what I want to see," she exclaimed. "There are customers lining up waiting for the store to open."

"Have you noticed anything special about this day?" asked Ray.

Lily stopped before unlocking the store's door. "When you first appeared," she answered, pensively, "I felt you were more than just another customer arriving the same as all the others. There was something unusual about you and the difference

137

was intriguing because this trait was felt but not immediately understood. Just now, you told me again you are more than just another customer. You are here for a purpose and with your question, the light of this morning brightened because, maybe, today I'll see how the pieces of life—and their purposes—fit together in the wider purpose of events. Our struggles are not just some things to be endured before we all die. There's a purpose to each life. It has a role in the sacred web. We can only try to understand why we are here. Most of it is to hone each person's spirit on the grindstone of trouble to improve ourselves on each obstacle. Such difficulties don't exist in the spirit world where we live; therefore we have to come to earth to improve. You, Raylon James, have a place in my future and, from your question, I can see today I'm about to discover why you are here at my store and this is not just to buy groceries."

"We are learning all the time," said Ray, "and from your long answer to my short question you have just told me again you, a descendant of countless generations of people living in what today we call Olympic National Park, see into the spirit world and always have had this ability. Missionaries, who first came to this region, thought only they had the answers for spiritual life and did not understand the people first to live on this land communicated with the Creator for thousands of years before the newcomers arrived. The newcomers looked at the first people to live here and did not see them."

"Maybe you could help bring new supplies into the store," said Lily. "First the small stuff then we must look into the present and the future."

"I have a list of things to get," added Ray. "Particularly, I want to include a bunch of those wondrous sandwiches and biscuits."

"OK," she replied, before they started to unload the car, bringing packages into the building.

After completing work with the bundles, Ray made some purchases, including additional sandwiches, biscuits and ice. He paid the bill and was about to relate his important information when Lily asked, "Can you stay for some coffee, I'm now going to get ready?"

"Of course," he replied, "and thanks."

When they were both holding paper cups filled with strongly scented drink, Lily said, "You asked if I had noticed anything special about today. I could not sleep last night because I was not tired but energized by beholding a spiritual light similar to a time when I received a vision. I again felt aware all things are connected and parts for some time separated would now come together, bringing a wondrous infusion of light, renewing our traditions. My name is Lily Gray Raven. My uncle Elijah Gray Raven phoned me this morning and told me to be ready for special information reminding me and others, all life is connected; thereby, in all the trouble, we are not alone. Parts once seeming to have been separated will come together again."

"I mentioned to you earlier," replied Ray, "I found a very old cabin structure up in a Sitka spruce. Now I have found a cave in the mountains. The cave is full of pounded coppers. Some are in the shape of shields. Mainly there are sheets of copper. On all these pieces, there are crests, symbols and, particularly, the narrative story of the Quinault people. Each item was signed by the name Gray Raven."

Lily screamed with her face brightening and light flashing in her eyes. "That's the message we have waited for through generations. Gray Raven, during his early years, as his first lifetime, had high status then he and his family members with him fell into disregard so he left the community, entering his second lifetime. He did not return. Our record keepers seemed to be certain in the future he, in some way, would restore lost prestige and this would return Gray Raven to our community, bringing great times to our whole family. I'm going to phone Eli now and tell him you are here and what you have found. He will, of course, want you to take him to the cave."

"I'm ready," stated Ray.

Lily made the call. The conversation was brief. Afterward, she turned to Ray and said, "He will be here soon."

By the time of a second cup of coffee, a truck stopped in front of the store. Lily and Ray hastened outside where a person stood, who at a first impression, seemed to be an average man. He was of medium height, slim with gray hair and shining dark eyes, which added a glow to his face. His depth of character became more fully revealed in the tone of his voice when he said, "Good morning, Lily. I should say great morning."

His voice had resonance, sounding as though it came from a vast storehouse of history and traditions. Not giving Lily time for introductions, the man turned to Ray and said, "You must be Ray James. I'm Eli Gray Raven. Could I ride with you as far as the trail goes? If I could leave my truck here, I'll be coming back with a crew. I have helpers and will call them from the cave. Lily, I'd like to buy some of your sandwiches and biscuits. I have packed coffee."

"Come on in," said Lily. "Sandwiches and biscuits are selling fast. I'm almost always out of them."

"If you weren't always out of them, I'd buy a lot more of them," added Eli.

Eli and Ray followed her into the building. Both men purchased supplies. Ray placed a package in his backpack then carried a parcel when all three people walked to his car. Eli placed his pack and walking stick on the back seat before he sat on the front passenger side. He closed the door, leaving the window open. After returning to the driver's place, Ray said to Eli, "Beautiful walking stick."

"I make then," replied Eli. "Each stick tells legends of our people."

To Lily, Ray said, "Thank you for the coffee. We'll see you soon."

"Thank you both for keeping our traditions," she replied, before Ray backed the car off the lot then turned onto the road.

"I haven't been this excited since I was a kid," exclaimed Eli.

"I don't know what I've found as well as you do but even with the smaller amount I know, I find this to be a special time," replied Ray.

"It is the return and third lifetime of my ancestor Gray Raven," said Eli. "Our family knew he was more than the rest of the community thought he was. We knew someday he would return and, when he did, he would restore our good name. I phoned another member of our family. When we have a location, I'll call him again and he will fly there. He has a tourist business and takes tourists on day trips. He also gives talks about the area while visitors are with him. This will be a great story to add to his list."

"Do you do the carvings on your sticks?" asked Ray.

"Yes," he replied. "You will notice an eagle, raven, bear, beaver and whale. I also work with others to carve canoes. My day job is being a ranger and interpreter—speaker—for the park. I'll have a plaque made, marking the cave as an historic site if it's in the park or not. Our traditions are here. They must be preserved, told and shared. You are part of our story. Events of such major importance don't happen by accident. This is the time for Gray Raven's return. You completed his story—our traditions. You are part of them."

"In our lives we don't foresee all the good and bad that will happen to us," observed Ray. "I came here to get stronger. This park, being ninety-five percent wilderness has brought out the wild and strength inside me, in my spirit. The strength was not outside but inside."

"I saw that in you when I met you," said Eli. "I'm proud to have you find the cave and be part of our story."

"That's greatly appreciated," exclaimed Ray. "I'm excited and proud to become part of your story. You and your family add traditions to Olympic National Park. We're at the end of the road. My camp is ahead."

Ray parked his car. Both men added containers of water along with Lily's sandwiches and biscuits to back packs. The travelers, each one with a walking stick, started a journey to recover the story of the last days of Gray Raven.

The next day, upon reaching the cave, Elijah Gray Raven was caught by the spell of what had been lost for so long. Walking a few steps along a trail into his past, a glow came over him, while he checked the traditions written in copper. Elijah phoned the crew and outlined the location of the discovery to get help bringing the past back to the present.

Ray shared some of his new friend's excitement. When the helicopter came into view, Ray said, "I've had a wondrous experience, finding first the cabin in the Sitka spruce and later the cave. Now I think this is my occasion to leave but I have enjoyed meeting you, Lily and your story."

"You are part of our story," replied Eli. "We will see you soon."

Ray started walking back to his camp. Reaching a high place on the trail, he looked back in time to see the copter land in front of the cave. Three men left the craft and greeted Elijah. Ray resumed his return journey.

When night's shadows gathered and darkened, the vague outlines of the trail became lost and Ray was forced to stop for the night. He gathered smaller sticks along with larger pieces to prepare a fire. It provided welcome warmth and light. To these basic comforts, he added the enjoyment of good food provided by Lily's sandwiches and biscuits. Afterward he relaxed just before the first wolf howled. *Old legends people did not know were here are being maintained,* thought Ray. *Now wolves, according to park brochures, not present during these recent times, seemed to have returned and call to this beautiful night with a sky filled with stars. First colors are appearing of a rising moon. I have entered a world, for a long time not known or seen. We are all enriched both by the restoration and presence of traditional life in addition to the natural world.*

In company with the past and present, Ray slept until light returned to brighten the landscape enabling him to travel again. *I'm proceeding slowly,* he said to himself. *While I approach the end of a long journey of discovery, I'm starting to notice something I've managed for a long time to ignore and that is fatigue. I'm approaching my camp on high ground of this mountain, both spiritually and physically and I have to rest.*

Upon reaching his camp, he stepped into the tent, got into the sleeping bag and welcomed the long ignored joy of sleeping. Hours later, he was awakened by calls of ravens. He selected all available pieces of food and left them on a flat rock within view of camp. The inquisitive and active birds quickly accepted the good start to a new day.

The park has a sensible policy of not feeding wildlife, thought Ray as he walked back to his tent. *I have a hunch I'm not in the park but ravens are smart and can remain wild while at the same time enjoy some treats. I also don't waste food.*

He kindled a fire in front of the tent before he unpackaged meat supplies he had purchased from Lily. At a point just above the flames, he prepared a skewer. On it he placed a section of freshly thawed Arctic char. While the meat sizzled and turned a dark golden color, Ray also unpacked a sandwich along with a biscuit. Lastly, he shared this last banquet with the ravens.

Following the finest of meals, he rested, watched sunlight draw colors out of objects previously not seen to have such beauty and recalled, *I have traveled a long way on an actual mountain route and much further into the past. Now I must pack and prepare to leave the mountains. In the evening, I like to, usually while sipping a beer, look back on the day and enjoy what was beautiful while also plan to, in the future, try to address needs now present. I equally enjoy the morning, when sipping coffee; I can look forward to the potential adventure provided by a new day. Without a plan there is only chaos. A lack of planning works for ravens because they do not have the choice of how to be better ravens. They just continue the way they are and have a good life as they have evolved to be adaptable. People don't have such a lack of choice. They must decide to follow the Creator and live their lives, making them better or turning away in a process of short-term gain but long-range darkness. I plan each day to stay on course because there is nothing chaotic about sacred life. The stars, moon, sun and earth all move by design. Our lives are planned. I think we plan them ourselves when we are in the spirit world and we visit earth to learn and develop from hardships that aren't present on the spiritual side, which people often call heaven. I came to a park to get strong. I selected Olympic National Park because it is the only park ninety-five percent wilderness. The wild clarified my view, enabling me to see that strength was present, not outside but inside. I had to recognize it, hone it and insert it more prominently into my character.*

Only after much work can we savor the joy of doing nothing and that's what I'm going to do today, decided Ray. True to his decision, he rested for the first occasion in a long time. Gradually, evening approached.

After adding more wood to the fire, Ray sat to watch sky and mountains beyond the flames. As flames grew taller they brightened the camp while seeming to bring increasing darkness to the outer landscape, where the setting sun was adding red hues. They, too, faded, leaving the night with only a remnant contrast of lighter sky and darker land. In front of both, flames moved while shadows danced. Ray looked back along the pageantry of a journey in himself, through the park. *I enjoy all three regions of this park, he concluded; however, at this time, before I leave I want to visit the coast again. I'll always miss the booming sound of swells as they move toward land, stand up, crest then crash with a sound that rumbles and becomes a most identifying song of the shore. Gulls add white specks to sky and land. A variety of animals walk the shore in their unending search for food. People go to the sea to enjoy its immensity and beauty while birds and animals enjoy life but don't seem to divide a day into segments. They don't become tourists but are almost always either searching for food or resting.*

In the temperate rain forest, birds sing among countless living parts, all growing in harmony with each other in an overall plan and connecting spirit of the Creator. The rain forest is the Creator's garden, breathing in and out. There are innumerable different parts connected as one life. Each single aspect contributes to all the others.

I also enjoy the mountains with towering forms of rock standing above clouds. I'll miss all three regions. Right now, before I sleep for the night, I want to hear calls of the wilderness.

They started as an almost unnoticeable, single, low cry. In numbers, depth and intensity, there developed, what Ray had hoped to hear. *The wilderness that calls out tonight,* he thought, *might just possibly include me.* Feeling his journey here to be complete, Ray started packing.

Next morning, when sunlight was hitting only the tops of mountains, Ray started traveling. This part of his journey brought him to a campsite near the shore where he could again go surfperch fishing. From nearby stores, he refurbished his supplies and, to them, added more cooking items along with beer and bait, consisting of razor clam necks and plastic sand worms.

Back at the campsite, he unpacked his supplies and prepared to go fishing the next day. When work was complete and snack finished, he sat to enjoy one of his favorite parts of a day. *I feel at home in all three regions of the park,* he recalled; *however I never feel as much a part of the place anywhere but by water. The larger the water gets, the more I seem to enjoy it. Sitting here at my camp, with a small fire in the pit, and just enjoying being here while I sip beer, I feel welcomed by the sound of the sea. Over and over again, the swells come to shore, rise up, crest then crash down with a great booming sound. Sitting here I can hear the boom of the sea although its presence is almost as noticeable by the scent of the air. Currents drifting in from the Pacific Ocean carry a scent of fish and salt. My camp along this shore reminds me of my home in Florida. Both are by the sea. I enjoy surfperch fishing because it's much the same as the way I fish in Florida. In this park, other surfperch fishermen use a two once, triangular, sand sinker at the end of the line with a hook up about two feet. That's the way I rig a line in Florida while other fishermen place a hook at the end of the line with a sinker up from the hook. I keep the hook off the bottom in an attempt to avoid bottom feeders such as stingrays and catfish.*

Next morning, the rising sun brought light to the landscape along with warmth and colors. Sky and water caught red hues, gradually fading, while the sun seemed to climb the sky. Among colors being replaced by golden light, Ray, wearing waders stepped into the surf. He had an external belt attached around his waist to keep the boots from completely flooding if he toppled into the water.

Ready to start fishing, he attached to a hook some razor clam necks then sent this bait far out to sink just behind churning water of a crashing wave. *Surfperch here are the same as sandpipers in Florida,* noted Ray. *Both search for food in the flow of water, after a wave has crashed.*

Hearing a person shout, Ray turned to watch a nearby fisherman carry a particularly large catch back to his car. When Ray's back was turned to the ocean, he heard a loud rushing of water before he was knocked over into crashing, very cold water. While thrashing, his boots touched solid ground and Ray stood up, bracing himself against any more unusually large swells. They did not appear. *Never turn your back on the sea,* recalled Ray. *I must remember all swells are not the same size. Some are much larger than others. In Hawaii, the Hawaiians would wait for large swells and let them carry the rafts to shore. I'm not just wet but very cold. There's also a large surfperch on the end of my line,* he noted before starting to reel in this outstanding catch. After placing the fish in a bag at his side, Ray sent the bait out again and in a short time had a second large fish to supply any fisherman a wonderful fish fry.

"That's how not to go surfperch fishing," said a neighboring fisherman, who had parked nearby and watched Ray's fishing procedures.

"If you can prove you can go under water to visit their world, the society of fish will send to you great catches," replied Ray.

"Oh," exclaimed the neighbor. "Turning your back on that large swell was just part of your technique."

"That's right," said Ray. "And you're the first one I've told about this method."

"I appreciate it," said the guy, laughing. "I won't try out your advice but I've enjoyed having you share it," said the guy, before he closed his car's trunk. "Been a great day already," he said, before walking toward the water."

"Any day we can go fishing is a special time," replied Ray.

After placing coverings over the car's seat to protect the area from wet clothing, he drove to his camp where he changed clothes, filleted fish and prepared to conclude a great day. When the aroma of frying surfperch drifted with air currents along with the usual blends of salt and fish, Ray eventually placed the golden fillets on a plate. To these special treats, he added malt vinegar, salt and pepper, before he sat to enjoy a great gift from the Pacific Ocean.

Good fish well-cooked is an unusual treat, he concluded, after enjoying the white colored, flaky fillets. He washed equipment then packed for the start of a new adventure.

Sitting in front of a small fire, enjoying the company of booming surf, he sipped beer and concluded; *I enjoy the feeling of being well organized. I came to this park to get strength. I selected this region because it is ninety five percent wilderness. In such an environment, I found the strength I needed. It was already present in me. I just had to make the discovery through being tested. Now, I can return home in my third lifetime, a period when I can face trouble when it comes. During my first lifetime, I had fun but wasn't tested. In my second lifetime I learned strength. Now I can face the future, tested sufficiently to look ahead knowing the world is a place of hard knocks and I can face them.*

From one point of view, I'm ready to leave Olympic National Park tomorrow. In reality, I know I never will leave. It will stay with me wherever I go. It won't become just a memory because its gift to me is lasting. Of all the parts of my great adventure at Olympic National Park, I'll best remember the people in addition to the great size and power of each of the three regions and always the booming of crashing waves or swells as they hit the shore.

The rising sun next morning found Ray leaving a donut shop. He carried a package of biscuits and a cup of coffee. He got back into his car, sat on the driver's seat then, with freshly acquired treats, he started returning home by the most direct route he could find. Leaving the park and Washington State, he drove into California then crossed into Nevada. He drove until he was too tired to proceed before getting a room then leaving the next morning. Enjoying seeing Joshua trees, which were actually cacti, he left Nevada, cut across part of

Utah and rested at Cameron, Arizona where he rented a room at the Cameron Trading Post. He welcomed, again, the site of the sturdy stone buildings steeped in southwestern style.

The restaurant portrayed the history of the area, as did the same lady Ray had met during his previous visit. She approached Ray after he sat at a table providing a view of the immense room. Similar to the other occasion, she wore a silver belt, silver and turquoise rings and a beaded broach neatly tying in place long black hair.

"Welcome back," she said. "Are you here to try again the Navajo taco?"

"You have an outstanding memory," replied Ray.

"I just recalled your other visit," she explained, "and anyone who tries the local favorite once will be back for more. Those things are addictive."

"Yes they are," he said. "The Cameron Trading Post is addictive."

The lady walked away but soon returned carrying a tall glass of water and another of draft beer.

"This place is special," said Ray. "What is your name?"

"Santee," she said. "And you are called?"

"Ray James," he said, before she returned to the kitchen.

After tasting some of the cold, clear water, he thought, *that might be overlooked in some places but I definitely notice it in a desert.*

He was sipping beer and trying to appreciate some of the story of the Navajo people presented in architecture when Santee appeared again carrying the taco feast. She placed the plate of food on the table and before walking away she observed, "Tourists order burgers. People of the community ask for the Navajo taco."

"Now there's a comment I enjoy even more than the taco and that's saying a lot," replied Ray.

Following Santee's departure, Ray looked at the display of food presented on the plate. On a large base of Navajo fry bread there was a thick topping of lean, ground beef, beans, chili, cheese, lettuce, and tomato.

Ray was sipping the last of the draft when Santee arrived and he said, "Fortunately, I have a room here because the local favorite could put a traveler to sleep for four years."

Laughing, she replied, "You will get some good dreams and maybe even a vision."

"I always enjoy visiting the Cameron Trading Post," he noted, after paying his bill and including a good tip.

Leaving the building he reentered the dry, clear, warm air of the desert. Nearby the Little Colorado River was being visited by numerous sheep. He entered his expansive, southwestern styled room designed to reflect the region where people and history had no choice but adapt to the prevailing desert. The land spoke of resistance to change. Traditions had strength and longevity. As night arrived, marked by the first then other howls of coyotes, Ray welcomed sleep.

When the sun was just appearing as a light in the east, Ray continued traveling. Accompanied by coffee and biscuits, he started a long journey, returning to his home in Florida. *Always driving with at least the driver's side window down,* he observed, *I think I would know when I had entered Florida by the air coming through my window. There is moisture, laced by scents of salt, fish and flowers. Florida belongs to the sea. Hawaii is another place of the sea, and there the fragrance of flowers fills the air.*

Chapter 4

The Third Life of Raylon James

Arriving back home in Florida, he parked the car on his driveway and thought; *someone has been looking after the place in my absence. Grass has been cut. Palms, flowers and borders are doing well.*

He entered the house and found the interior to be just as it was when he left. Mail had been placed on a table. He looked out the windows and saw waves moving toward shore as if he had not been missed and his absence had gone unnoticed. *I have the strangest feeling that my departure has made a difference only to myself,* he reflected.

Work first and play later has always been my policy, he remembered, before he walked outside. He stopped, looked around and enjoyed seeing again all the features he had not seen for so long. The greatest shock came when he looked up on the roof. From the top of the building, the heron and egret watched him. "How did you know?" he asked them. "I've been away a long time but you are here to greet me when I return. Welcome back."

I was wrong before, he thought. *Someone did miss me; but how did they know when to come back so they would be here at the exact time of my arrival. Someone told them—a friend we both have in common.*

He started unloading the car, putting everything in its place. Through this process, he noted his need to purchase some supplies. At nearby stores, he replaced the missing items in addition to getting a takeout burger and juice.

Back at his house, he was again watched while he unpacked. He put away the new supplies, enjoyed the snack and, after all necessary projects had been completed; he walked to rejoin the companionship of the sea. At the shore, he sat on a stretch of dray sand and recalled, *I didn't feel totally at home when I moved back into the house. It is a place of shelter but made of inanimate wood, glass and cement. I enjoy the memories of home but am less tied to the structure of the building, although I value its association to good memories. My home is really out here and the best part is in the wondrous reality that the water realm, including shoreline has not changed. Thereby I can return to life as it was and continues to be. I could tell the time of day by colors of it. According to paleness of sky and placement of sun, the day is presently about an hour passed noon.*

Porpoises continue to swim a short distance out from shore. A soft breeze brings freshness to dispel heat, while sending waves toward the sand. Here, they curl upward and catch flashes of light from the sun just before crashing down to form long, white strands of churning water. They become flows streaming over sand until meeting a high point where they are turned back to move under the next crest. Like surfperch chasing food in churning water behind swells moving to shore, sandpipers hunt food in streams of water swirling across sand.

There is life here, noted Ray, *and that's what I enjoy the most. This place is more than a collection of random parts. There is a spirit of life here, making each single component more than just a porpoise, a turtle, or fish. Porpoises, a long way back in time were hippos. Gradually they lived more in water and left their connection to land except for their necessity to swim up through the surface to breathe. Whales and manatees have the same connections.*

Ray started walking along the beach following the border of firm sand between crashing waves and dry sand. The breeze moved a few clouds in a blue sky where a frigate bird watched the realm below. Pelicans patrolled the water, soaring above the waves.

As I travel along the beach, he thought, *the enjoyment of environment returns to me like meeting again an old friend. Memories and enjoyments also flash back, as I enter the song of the sea. There is the sound of water splashing, wind stirring, and leaves moving*

He kept walking, remembering the wilderness of Olympic National Park. *The park has three areas,* he recalled. *They are ocean, forest and mountains. Here in Florida, the wilderness of the sea comes up to the land where there continues to be sections remaining natural. The wild of Olympic National Park enabled me to find, in myself, the strength I sought. Troubles will come. Now, I know I have the strength to face them. I'll stand up to each one and carry on until one defeats me and that will be my last battle. We all have a final struggle. I don't see mine on the horizon yet.*

Ray turned around and started walking back along the beach. He now pushed into a slight breeze, which had been at his back, previously.

That's beyond anything I could possibly have imagined to be true and one of the most amazing wildlife experiences I've encountered, thought Ray, when he looked at his side and, moving slightly to soar into the oncoming breeze, there was the great blue heron with wings fully outstretched to keep up-lifted. *The majestic heron is gliding beside me.*

I would not have believed this, if I were not seeing it, exclaimed Ray in thought, *but it is occurring. The heron and egret met me when I got home. Now, the heron soars beside me. Likely, the snowy egret will meet us up ahead where we go fishing. For the birds and with them, I'll have to go fishing.*

While the birds waited on the beach, Ray walked to his house, got his fishing equipment and returned. On the sand, he placed a bucket for minnows. From a tall pail, he removed a throw net. Next he put in place a folding chair before leaning his fishing pole on it.

The two birds knew the routine and displayed excitement in their own ways. They watched intently as each piece of equipment dropped into place. Interest intensified when the net left the pail to be carried into the water. He shook the mesh folds out so the netting dropped neatly downward, held in place by sinkers. One section followed by another was gathered up before an outward toss unraveled the net bordered by a circle of sinkers. This trap dropped into the water and vanished just before moving to shore where silvery-sided minnows fell from the net and dropped into the bucket along with surrounding sand. The feast started until each bird seemed to be sufficiently full to walk away and watch for the next adventure.

Ray placed one of the small, silvery fish on a hook, positioned up from a sinker at the end of the line. The equipment was carried out to deeper water before the fish was tossed out to even greater depths then came the time of waiting at shore until the pole throbbed.

The birds are watching the pole as closely as I am, observed Ray. To his friends, he said, "You met me when I got home. People have devices to keep informed on traveling times and other information. You have none of these physical devices; yet you met me. You could only have received information from our friend. Everything is connected. The one who connects us all keeps different parts working in harmony; people have the means to disrupt that harmony because of freedom of choice. The heron and egret don't have the choice of turning away from the Creator."

The pole slammed down toward the water, sending all three fishermen into action. Ray started trying to reel in line as the other two watched and waited. Slowly a long, streamlined king mackerel came to shore where Ray had to help the birds get a share. "I don't always fillet at the beach," he said to the birds, "because sand sometimes gets on the meat; sharing means working here."

While fillets were prepared other pieces were thrown to the birds. Parts the birds could not use were placed in a bag to go into dumpsters at the back of the motel ready for pickup in the morning. Ray carried fillets along with the equipment to his house.

First, he put away the equipment. One piece of meat was placed with water in a bag to be saved in the freezer. A remaining slab was dropped into a bag containing corn meal then placed in a hot, oiled pan. The fillet sizzled, sending out unmistakable fragrances of cooking food from the sea.

Now I'm home, observed Ray, after he had savored the crisp, white, flaked food, his first meal from the Gulf, since he had returned. Afterward, he cleaned the kitchen, sat back in his favorite chair to look out the windows to the water and watch evening approach, as he reluctantly gave in to sleep.

Next morning, while a mockingbird was singing, Ray entered one of his favorite restaurants and ordered a special meal of pancakes. *This place is similar to a journey back in time,* he thought, as the server, Laura, poured a second cup of coffee. Her hair was black although graying and the rest of her presence seemed built to be functional rather than beautiful.

"This place never changes and you don't either," said Ray, bringing a smile to her face.

"We're stuck in time," she said, laughing. "I can't leave because, if I do, I'll age by fifty years."

"You don't get older," replied Ray. "You just gather memories."

"Thank you," she said, "and you, I remember, even without the kind comments. Strange though, how other customers seem to all look alike after a while, just as the days of my life; I don't notice time passing, except when my age keeps getting higher."

"Being in place is better than being out of place," he concluded.

"That's the good part of my life," she stated, as her face brightened.

"We are here to improve ourselves," noted Ray. "Advancement can come suddenly, through hard knocks or gradually, through time. "You seem to be getting better day-by-day, rather than through dramatic hardship. You are lucky."

"Thanks," she said. "I hadn't thought of it that way. I have always been worried I've been comfortable here but wasting my time. You have shown me a better interpretation."

Bringing the pancakes, Laura said, "I hope you have as wonderful a day as you have made mine."

"You're an essential part of a great restaurant," he replied. "I feel as much at home here as I do at my own house."

"Your house is here in Florida?" she asked, surprised.

"Yes," he answered.

"Whether you were a tourist or resident, I always felt you belonged here," she explained.

"After I've been traveling, I always relax when I return to Florida," he observed.

"Welcome back," she said, before walking away to greet arriving customers.

That makes three, he mused. *I've been welcomed back by a heron, egret and now, Laura. Of course, I've always felt I was part of the environment, here or at Olympic National Park. There is a presence, spiritual connection, to land, water and sky, which goes beyond the physical. From the sacred, we can't get away. There is no such thing as tourist or holiday. Series of days are part of one life regardless of where the days occur.*

Cold pancakes, accompanied by cold coffee completed the meal. Ray returned to his house and answered to the call of the Gulf. He walked the beach, joining the song of sky, water and land. Waves crashed along shore as they always did, even when they could only be heard at night from the house. Sandpipers chased flows of water, looking for

173

food such as coquinas. The slight breeze seemed to be always present, bringing to shore a refreshing blend of fragrances, particularly of fish, salt and, sometimes, flowers.

I can tell where I am by the air, observed Ray. *Florida has air from the water and this is a dominant presence. In Hawaii, also a place in the sea, the strongest presence in the air is perfume from flowers.*

Enough of walking and dreaming, decided Ray. *I have friends to feed.*

The heron and egret watched Ray collect and put into place his fishing equipment. After the birds had been given their first treats, he baited his hook then waded into the water. Deeper areas were darker blue while green and yellow hues tinted shallow sections. Sunlight outlined numerous mullet swimming past.

Ray went back to shore, got the net and with one throw caught some mullet and extra sardines known as greenbacks. He took this treasure to the sand where two herons and the egret enjoyed a feast. Following this meal, one of the herons issued a squawk, stretched out broad wings and climbed the sky, traveling to a site known only in the world of birds.

"I haven't had just one great blue heron for a companion," said Ray, to the one remaining. "You are actually a pair of herons and you take turns being on the beach."

The birds, observed Ray, *can't take any more food yet they remain because such an activity is their life. They are part of the sky, sand and water. Looking for food is what they do.*

This is what I enjoy doing, he thought, as he sat and watched the landscape, while his pole kept in place a baited line stretching out into blue depths. *I like to sit and watch the world. In the morning, evening, or when I'm fishing, I stop and question what I'm doing. I'm back now to the place of my first lifetime, when life was fun almost all the time. I was as a person on vacation, just seeking enjoyments. A wakeup call came when I met a wall of a washroom because Cal Hooper had thrown me there then dumped me out among garbage pails. Clearly, I needed strength and went to Olympic National Park*

175

to find it. In the park's wilderness I found what I sought. It was not outside of me but inside. Strength was there, I just had to become aware of it and that process brought me to my present, third lifetime. Now, with strength, I can face the world.

I remember the way things were. The sky is almost always blue. Clouds drift past. A slight breeze usually sends to shore waves as sandpipers search for food. Backs of porpoises break through the water; during the quest these animals follow a short distance out from shore. Pelicans patrol the water as if that was their one purpose in life. Sometimes, a frigate bird seems to hang in the sky or a crab boat will come into view while fishermen check their traps.

Seeing birds jump with excitement and the fishing pole bend into a partial circle, Ray sprang into action, picked up the pole and felt the force of a large fish fighting against the line. *The struggle is always exciting as the prize is uncertain,* thought Ray, while he struggled to wind in line as it moved across the water, following the fish.

The excitement ended when Ray brought to shore a large king mackerel. To his watching friends,

Ray said, "We all caught our limits today. The water provides and always will if we fish respectfully and take according to what is available and not more than we need." Ray carried his catch-of-the-day to his house. The birds flew to its roof.

I entered the wilderness at Olympic National Park and can stay with the wild here, thought Ray, as he removed chunks of coral from a border outlining a section of hibiscus flowers. *The wild is inside me and so is the strength I sought. The person who traveled to the park is not the same as the one who returned. I have really just become more aware of who I am. I have the wild in me and I know I'm strong.*

Ray placed the coral chunks in a circle around what would be a fire pit he prepared in front of his house. The circle of coral was also ideally placed at the top of the slope leading to the beach. Having established a fire pit and placed skewers for cooking, he walked to the beach and collected driftwood for burning.

When all preparations had been completed, he looked around at his home and thought, *a new life begins. After I establish a steady firebase, I'll prepare the fillets for a meal.*

To fine kindling, he brought a match's flame. The fire at first seemed to hesitate before swarming though dry twigs to climb larger pieces of wood. Brightness of the fire caused the surrounding landscape to appear darker. Beyond the fire, a last flash of light from the setting sun painted sky and water with hues of red before all color faded with advance of night's shadows. The sound of waves continued to come from the beach.

The meat was positioned on a skewer in heat just above the flames. Cooking progressed rapidly, while Ray got from his house a paper plate accompanied by plastic knife and fork. He also had basic additions of salt, pepper and malt vinegar.

He placed the golden fillet of roasted food on the plate, spread the toppings then sat down to enjoy one of the finest meals from the sea. For a drink, he had a glass of what had become a representative of Florida and that was juice from an orange grove.

Following the meal, he burned remaining parts before he walked to the house and returned with a tall glass of beer. He sat down, sipped beer and watched the wilderness of the sea as it came up to the shore. *Florida is a wild place,* he thought, *because the Gulf is a wilderness. It borders the land, bringing this wild presence right up to the cities. Nothing escapes from the water. The sea prevails and, during the worst storms, the water will show its dominance over cities. The air belongs to the ocean with its identifying scents of salt and fish. Almost always, a breeze blows from the vastness of the water to the land.*

The moon is now rising, returning color taken away by the setting sun. At first there are all shades of red. They fade while the moon rises to gradually become a bright orb, coating sky and water with a glow of silver. A path of light flows from the moon to my fire; all people would see a path of light forming a trail to them. We are important although we don't always feel to be. We often wonder how such a thing could be true; but there are times, flashes of light, as a silver trail to the moon, when each person could see every part is important and guided.

179

On shore, people keep clearing away the natural areas, not realizing they are removing the Creator's garden and chipping away at the spirit world, where each person is connected forever, unless they turn themselves away and bring about their own darkness.

At home with the wild, Ray slept in his chair beside the fire. It reduced to coals then embers before the next new day was announced with the rising sun. It awakened Ray, who first saw the Gulf then the heron and egret watching him from the roof of the house.

He walked to the beach, threw out the net and brought back minnows and a few mullet to feed the birds. He also saved minnows for future use. They would be kept in the freezer until needed by birds or for bait.

Having taken care of the birds, he drove to a restaurant and brought back a takeout breakfast consisting of pancakes with the toppings along with Florida's trademark of the finest orange juice. Lastly, there was coffee.

Following the meal, he sat in his favorite chair inside his house and watched his view of the world as it always included the Gulf. As a gust of Gulf breeze entering Ray's world, this presence opened the back door, walked into the house and stood in front of Ray.

He was shocked while not being all that much surprised. At first glance, Mylee Clandon seemed to be much the same as she had been. She was slim, with blue eyes and dark blonde hair.

To Mylee, the house appeared to be much as she had left it during her inspection tours while Ray was away. Ray, too, seemed unchanged other than now he was present. His black hair contained more gray. His greenish-blue eyes shocked her because of the extra spirit she saw there. He was much the same but he had also changed.

"Sit down," he suggested, before he shared with her a cup of black coffee.

"Thank you," she replied, receiving the drink then sitting on her usual chair. "While you were away, I looked after the place. That's what I intended to do now and was pleasantly shocked to see your car in the driveway."

"The place looks great, just the way we left it," he observed. "I hoped the person taking care of everything was you."

"Am I still welcome here?" she asked.

"I wasn't the one who left you," he countered.

"I didn't leave you," she stated.

"How did we get where we are now?" he asked.

"Cal Hooper said you got sick at the bar and went home," she explained. "He said you had asked him to see that I was all right and to give me a ride home. On the way back, he showed me his oyster bar. A job was available there and an apartment to go with it so I tried it out for a while and constantly tried to keep you up-dated but I could not contact you. When I went to the house, as I have kept doing, you seemed to have gone but would be back. I waited for your return. Cal's true character came to light and during one of our arguments, after I told him I was leaving, he told me the truth of what had happened at the bar. He also hit me. That's a line with me no guy ever crosses. I left and started working at another oyster bar I now own. I've been staying there. I've looked for you every day and taken care of this property, waiting for your return. As I said, he told me what had happened at the restaurant where he knocked you out and left you outside with the garbage. After that, you went away. I was sure you would come back. Now you have returned. I hope you can forgive me for all of my mistakes. I did not think you would be away so long. I kept waiting and looking after the house that, before this all happened, I thought was our home and we would be confirming this soon with a ring."

"As I mentioned before," explained Ray, "I wasn't the one who left you. At the restaurant-bar, I woke up at the back among the garbage pails. Cal Hooper had met me in the washroom, explained that all people we work with are not friends and he wanted you. There was a fight during which he slammed me against the washroom wall, knocked me out then dumped me back with the garbage. You have just said he told you I wanted him to take you home because I was leaving. I had not left. I was out with the garbage and greeted the next morning by raccoons. They are related to bears and I was pleased to be surrounded with raccoons rather than bears. I returned to the house and realized I had to get some strength to face troubles of the world, such as the Cal Hoopers. To find strength, I knew the place to look was in the wilderness of the national parks. I chose Olympic National Park because it is ninety-five percent wilderness. I went there and entered the wild as it entered me. I also was helped to see the strength I sought was already in me and all I had to do was become aware of this presence and add it to my self-awareness. Now I have the strength I sought. The wilderness took me to itself and I took the wild into me. I've not changed but just rearranged who I always was. So I'm the same. I hope you are too. Welcome home. I thought you had left and I'm pleased to see you are back."

"Wow," she replied, before taking a long drink of cold coffee. "My actions might have looked as though I was leaving but I thought everything had your approval because Cal Hooper said you asked him to give me a ride home. You didn't say to take a job at his oyster bar but I kept trying to contact you about that. You left. I looked after the place until you came back. The only thing that has changed with me is I was lied to. My mistake was in not checking more carefully what I was being told; a good lesson in life. If you can forgive me, we can go back to the way we were."

"That's the way I thought things were in the past and the way I see them now," replied Ray.

"That's a relief to me," she said. "I was nervous when I came in here; but now I feel better. My life is back."

"Welcome home," he said, laughing. "It's too early in the day but could I pour you one of your favorite margaritas?"

"By the time shown on a clock this is early in the day but, considering the worry I've had and now have lost, the day has been long and I would really appreciate a celebration with a margarita," she stated.

After preparing the drinks, Ray gave one to Mylee before he sat and said, "I traveled a long distance but mainly the journey was inside myself."

Seeing Mylee sitting again on her favorite chair, Ray felt the light she shone into his life had returned. "When I drove onto the driveway and parked the car," he explained, "I was pleased to see signs the place was being looked after and hopefully by you. As I walked into the house, everything seemed to be in place. I had attained awareness of myself but had I lost my home? At first glance, all parts appeared to be in order and nothing had changed until you walked in. You returned a glow that was temporarily missing. Now everything is complete. I can't tell you fully how pleased I am to see you return. I hope you will stay."

Tears dampened her face. She wiped them away with her hand, sipped some margarita and looked out the windows to the Gulf before she said, "A cloud has cleared away from me. I'm free again. I'm home. That's what has happened to me and you have told me about your amazing journey of self-discovery. Welcome to a new lifetime—your third. I always felt you did not leave; so I looked after the place, waiting for you to come back."

"Leaving was not my intention," he replied. "Self-healing was my destination and, having been restored, I am home. We should celebrate. Would you like to go back to the restaurant where so many events started?"

"We'll go back there if you want to," she stated, seeming to collect words carefully before sipping more margarita. "I could leave that place in the past. We've traveled beyond it."

"I leave much in the past, also," he agreed. "Progress happens best when we are not dragging a lot of unnecessary baggage. I can overlook what Cal Hooper did to me because I have, with spiritual help, worked through it to a better understanding. I don't overlook the trouble he caused you."

Ray sipped some draft then looked around at his new home. Seeing it complete again, added a glow to the joy he felt about just being home. "Nothing is as it was before because my self-awareness has been re-assessed. We never would go back the same way again although we could return to that restaurant. It used to be our favorite place for celebrating."

"Do you want to drive?" she asked.

"Your choice," he replied.

"You can drive," she said. "I would enjoy being a passenger for a change."

Walking out to Ray's car, Mylee said, "The birds left when you were away. I notice they are back—on the roof."

"I don't notice them coming and going because when I'm here they are always present," explained Ray.

"I would really prefer to not go back to that particular place," said Mylee, while she sat on the passenger's seat as Ray started driving toward the restaurant.

"If you firmly decide you don't want to do this, we won't ever go back," stated Ray. "I don't overlook the way Cal Hooper treated you."

After Ray parked the car on a lot, they entered the restaurant. Mylee led the way to the same table they had used during the visit from Cal Hooper.

Drinks arrived, followed by a meal when Mylee said, "He has a lot o' nerve to ever try to talk to us again. Cal is here. He's approaching our table."

"I can't believe it," exclaimed Cal. "Are you back for more of what you got the last time?"

"That's not even possible," answered Ray as he stood up. He landed a punch on Cal's face, stunning him. A second blow to the other side of his face left him with a mainly blank look on his face.

Ray got a solid grip on the guy's shirt and jacket, hauled him to the bar, picked him up and threw the guy over the counter. He landed amid an explosion of falling and breaking bottles.

In silence so intense the tapping of his shoes could clearly be heard, Ray returned to the table and sat again across from Mylee.

"I didn't want to come back here," said Mylee, as her face brightened with a smile, "but I'm so glad we did. I wouldn't have missed this for anything. To all the bullies in the world," she added as she held up her glass, "may they all fall in a pile of rubble as I saw here today, with the fall of Cal Hooper. This should not be seen as an isolated event but part of justice in life."

There was some stirring of broken glass when two security men helped Cal stand then slowly leave the restaurant. When the men returned, they started to clean up debris around the bar. "I'd like to think I could've done that myself," said one man to the other.

"I agree," said the second guy. "Would've felt better doin' it rather than watchin' it but I enjoyed it anyway."

"Yeah," exclaimed the other guy. "So did I."

Leaving their work, the two employees walked over to the table where Ray and Mylee were sitting and one of them said, "Thanks for the action. That should've been done a long time ago. I regret I didn't do what you did but Len and I enjoyed it anyway and came over to thank you."

"Thank you," replied Ray. "I did it for my wife—girlfriend. He harmed her.

The men walked away leaving behind Mylee with a smile as noticeable as the light in her face. "Wife?" she asked.

"If you say yes," he answered.

"You have to ask first," she replied, enjoying his discomfort.

"Don't put me through that," he said.

190

"You can come here and do battle and it doesn't bother you at all but to show any kind of feeling for me, you panic," she stated.

"That's accurate," he agreed. "Will you marry me?" he asked, relieved to maybe have finished his part.

"I'll have to think about it," she replied, enjoying the moment.

Following enough silence, she said, "Yes, of course. I said that a long time ago over and over again."

"It's the formalities that I'm uncomfortable with," he explained.

"I know," she said. "We could take care of them quickly.

"Thank you," he exclaimed.

"I hope you are always as right as you were about coming here today," she stated, while they walked to a counter where Ray paid the bill.

Ray said to the woman at the counter, "I'll pay for the damages."

"There are no damages," she replied. "That dustup has been a long time coming."

When Ray and Mylee were leaving the restaurant, she said, "Not the same as our previous visit."

"The difference in the two visits, he replied, "was a journey to Olympic National Park."

About The Author

Daniel Hance Page is a writer with over thirty books published and others being written. His books are authentic stories filled with action, adventure, history, and travel including Indigenous traditions and spiritual insights to protect our environment in the smallest park or widest wilderness.

Made in the USA
Columbia, SC
07 January 2023

75557697R00107